Swallowing
the Sun

Terry Trueman

Hodder
Children's
Books

a division of Hodder Headline Limited

A Catalogue record for this book is available
from the British Library

ISBN 0 340 86641 1

Typeset in Bembo by Avon DataSet Ltd,
Bidford-on-Avon, Warwickshire

Printed and bound in Great Britain by
Bookmarque Ltd, Croydon, Surrey

The paper and board used in this paperback by
Hodder Children's Books are natural recyclable products
made from wood grown in sustainable forests.
The manufacturing processes conform to the environmental
regulations of the country of origin.

Hodder Children's Books
a division of Hodder Headline Limited
338 Euston Road
London NW1 3BH

About the Author

I've b...
old. Pe..pl...
about pe..pl...
   I live in the inl...d ...
of Spokane, Washington. ...
most of the time and enjo, ...
SWALLOWING THE SUN is inspired b...
San Pedro Sula Honduras in the early 1980s.

Praise for *Stuck in Neutral*

HIGHLY COMMENDED
NASEN Special Educational Needs Book Awards

COMMENDED
Sheffield Children's Book Award

'An intensely moving autobiography of adolescent angst and supreme loneliness. It's an impressive book, harrowing to read, and very difficult to forget.' Marilyn Brocklehurst, Norfolk C...dren's Book Centre

'An extraordinary journey into the landscape of someone else's mind . . . a real page-turner.' Lyn Gardne.. Book of the Month in *The Guardian*

'Extraordinary, prize-winning novel . . . a page-turning thriller as well as a celebratory book about simple pleasur..s.' *The Sunday Times*

Also by Terry Trueman

Stuck in Neutral

Other titles published by Hodder Children's Books

Dead Negative
Control-Shift
Seed Time
Nick Manns

Heathrow Nights
Jan Mark

Light
Alan Davidson

Sea Hawk, Sea Moon
Beverley Birch

Blackthorn, Whitethorn
The Flight of the Emu
THE MOVING TIMES TRILOGY:
Bloom of Youth
Grandmother's Footsteps
Stronger than Mountains
Rachel Anderson

Shadow of the Beast
Owl Light
Dark of the Moon
Maggie Pearson

For Jesse Cruz Trueman

MARCH 1998

It's early on a Saturday morning in our little town of La Rupa, but I'm with a beautiful girl on the beach at Omoa. She looks at me, and smiles, very sexy. Now she whispers, 'Jose,' in a strangely deep voice.

'JOSE!' The voice whispers again, but when I open my eyes the girl is gone. My older brother Victor wakes me up with a rough jerking of my shoulder.

'Hurry up!' Victor snaps, giving me the 'shush' sign, so that I won't wake up our little brother Juan sleeping in his bed across the room.

Victor drags me into our backyard before I even have any breakfast. I'm grumpy and not real happy, but of course he couldn't care less about my mood.

Victor's decided he wants to build a brick barbecue for our parents; it'll be an anniversary gift. Mom likes to cook outside, since the days and evenings are warm and humid, and cooking over a small fire-pit in the backyard beats standing at the stove in a hot kitchen. Nearly every family has a barbecue pit; we've always had one.

But Victor has decided that he wants to build a *brick* barbecue – and not just any brick barbecue. And when Victor decides something, that's pretty much that.

The minute we start, I can tell that we have very different thoughts about how to do this job. When

Victor first talked to me about this, last night, I figured it would take an hour or so this morning. But I can see that's not the way it's going to go. Victor's already prepared the site, just outside the back door of our house. He's leveled the ground, put down a layer of sand and clay and sprayed it damp.

I ask, 'How big are you going to make this?'

Victor is laying out the first layer of bricks, the foundation, and it spans an area five feet deep by seven feet long.

'This big,' Victor answers, pointing at these bricks he's laid out.

'Victor,' I whine, 'it'll look more like a house than a barbecue!'

'It has to be big, we're a big family,' he says, his voice dropping to a slightly lower, menacing tone; when Victor's voice gets low, it's best to just back off, but I can't stop myself.

I ask, 'How high is it going to go?'

'About here,' Victor says, holding his hand out at the level of his shoulders.

Biting my lip and turning my head away so that he won't see me laugh, I say, 'But Mom won't even be able to reach the top to cook on it.'

Victor, his tone even lower, holds his hand at waist level and says, 'The *grill* will be this high, idiot!' Now, he lifts his hand back up to the height of his shoulders again, 'the back of the barbecue will come up to here.'

'Victor,' I speak softly, 'why does it have to be so huge?'

Victor stops working and turns towards me, the ultimate danger sign. 'This is how they build barbecues all over the world, preppy-boy. They make them out of brick and they build them to last. This is for our parents and our family. It's going to be the biggest and the best barbecue in all of La Rupa. Your friends from your little rich-kid school can come here and Mom can cook on this. It'll be great. Now, that's enough *stupid* questions. Don't bother me again. Just keep bringing over those bricks.'

Last week, Victor brought home a huge load of red bricks from a factory being torn down in San Pedro Sula, the big city thirteen miles east of La Rupa. I'm sure the reason Victor wants to build something this size is because he has all these free bricks and is determined to use them. Of course Victor, being Victor, comes up with a plan to build the most grotesque and ridiculously oversized barbecue in the history of Central America.

'Get to work, Preppy!' he barks at me.

Victor's always been a little jealous of me going to a bilingual school (Spanish/English). He calls me 'preppy-boy' or 'preppy' when he wants to tease me. He doesn't understand that I kind of like these nicknames. I'm not going to say that Victor is crazy and impossibly bull-headed. I'm not going to say that – but that doesn't mean it's not true!

I want to tell Victor that people in other parts of the world don't build huge brick barbecues anymore. I want to tell Victor that a five foot by seven foot by five foot tall brick barbecue just out the back door of our house is too much. I try to think of excuses to change Victor's mind: this monstrosity will block the sun and ruin the younger kids' health. It will embarrass us in the eyes of our neighbors. Already, Mr Arroyos who lives with his wife in the back of their little store across the street is out sweeping his porch like he does every morning. He's a funny, smart, nice guy but when he glances in our direction he has to hide his laughter. I want to tell Victor that if his barbecue falls down it will kill us all. I want to say *anything* I can to get Victor to come to his senses – but because I want even more for Victor not to *murder* me, I keep my mouth shut and just keep working. I am thirteen years old and Victor is seventeen. He is the master. I am the slave. Some things are as hard as bricks.

Throughout the day, as hour after hour drags on, we begin to gather a crowd of neighbors along the street, watching us work. It starts with the kids but, eventually, parents come over too. We have quite an audience; the Arroyos, right across the street, lean out of the window of their little store and smile at us. Vera Ramerez, who lives next door, cooks bacon and eggs in a skillet over her little fire in her backyard. Eventually, whole families, all of La Rupa, show up: the Handels, the Ortegas, the Baronas, the Altunez, Mr and Mrs Cortez, the Barabons, and everyone else, at one time or another during the long day, wander by to watch us.

'Hey Victor, that's quite a structure,' says Mr Ramerez, smiling, 'only I'm not sure La Rupa needs a jailhouse.' Victor forces a laugh.

As I am picking up a load of bricks, Allegra Barabon calls to me, 'Jose!' I glance over and see her twirling one of her pig-tails around her finger. 'Do you feel like a mule?' I don't answer but I force a smile at her joke.

Victor's huge barbecue has become the day's major entertainment attraction.

Our sister Ruby, who is sixteen years old and the unofficial beauty queen of the town, comes out and watches us too.

Ruby says, teasingly, 'My goodness Victor, you are truly the brick barbecue building king of all Honduras.' She looks over at our crowd of neighbors and smiles, then she says to Victor, 'As you can see, such talent does not go unrecognized nor unappreciated!' Our neighbors smile back at Ruby, and Victor laughs. If I said the same things she is saying, I'd be dead! Later, Ruby brings us glasses of lemonade, which I sip slowly. Victor inhales his in one gulp.

Dad comes out of our house and sees all our neighbors standing around. He walks over and visits for a while with Mr Barabon and Mr Cortez. When Dad comes back by us he comments on what a 'substantial' barbecue it will be, and Victor seems very proud. But when Dad sees that Victor isn't looking, he winks at me.

I try to pretend this isn't really happening. I see the flock of wild parrots that live in the trees behind La Rupa, soaring overhead; they're so graceful. I look up at the steep, green hill that rises along the north side of town; I've always felt that this hillside is a wall; a lush, safe, green wall protecting us from the world. I smell the smoke of breakfast fires around town, especially from next door where Mrs Ramerez has finished cooking. She looks over at me and smiles giving me a thumbs-up sign. I manage to smile back in spite of how tired I feel. I've known Vera Ramerez since I was born. She's like a second mother. Some of the kids, led by Carlos and Pablo Altunez, tire of watching us and go out in the street and play soccer. I can't stop and join them. Victor would never allow that, but as I carry bricks I see all the houses of our little town. Glancing at our neighbors who stand talking together, watching Victor and me, I know every home in La Rupa, the colors, shapes and sizes of every room, and I know every person in every home. I know where they sleep, where they eat, who gets along or doesn't get along with one another, I could even tell you who washes his hands and who doesn't after he's used the toilet (there aren't many secrets in a place this small).

The only family I don't know – a family no one in town wants to know – are the Rodriquez, squatters living on the opposite side of town from our house.

They moved here a few months ago, poor people with three kids and no money. Their 'house' is made of cardboard, plastic tarps and a few scraps of weathered plywood. Every neighborhood and small town in Honduras has at least one 'Rodriquez' family.

Finally, seven hours after we started, my hands raw and sore, Victor all hunched over, we are nearly finished. A murmur spreads throughout the town and soon all of our neighbors, most everyone in La Rupa, come back to watch Victor apply the last brick. When it's perfectly in place, Victor says to me, 'That's it.' All of our neighbors, our audience, burst into applause. They call out, teasing, 'Bravo!' 'Bravo!' 'Encore!'

Angelina Altunez, Carlos and Pablo's mom, says, 'Aren't you going to name it, Victor?' Victor wouldn't let our neighbors see him blush but, ignoring her question, he smiles, raises his arms and takes a dramatic bow, which makes everyone laugh, cheer and applaud even louder.

My shirt is soaked with sweat. I am filthy and can't even stand up straight, but at least we're finally finished. The barbecue is truly amazing, huge and solid and completely overblown. As Victor and I walk slowly back towards our house, I overhear someone, one of the adult men, mention a name for the barbecue, 'Victor's Folly . . .'

I glance over at Victor, but he's walking several steps ahead of me and is almost into our house already; he doesn't hear this remark.

Victor's Folly, huh?

What about *me*?

SIX MONTHS LATER:
OCTOBER 4, 1998

One

Only five of us are home for dinner tonight. I ask one of my sisters, Maria, in English, to pass me a tortilla. This sounds like a poem because 'Maria' rhymes with 'tortilla'. Anyway, as I ask her I get sort of a kick out of my cleverness. The wind is blowing hard, the sound of it roars through our little house. Maria either ignores me or doesn't hear. With her you can never tell. Why doesn't she do a poem back at me, something like, 'No way, Jose . . . You'll get no tortilla from Maria!'?

'Maria,' I ask again, raising my voice, 'will you please pass me a . . .'

I don't finish my sentence because in this instant the monster lands on our roof with a terrifying, enormous thud. Our house shudders under the weight of him.

There is a terrible creaking. It feels as if the skeleton of our home, the frame itself will give way and collapse. My mother, walking back towards the table from across the kitchen, freezes in her tracks, as still as a statue. It's as though Mom thinks any movement on her part will signal to the monster that our family is here. My baby brother, Juan, and my youngest sister, Angela, stare up at the ceiling. They, too, can feel the weight of the beast sitting there.

Maria looks at me and asks, 'What?' She is the only person in our house who has not noticed the monster.

'Shush,' I say to her quickly, holding my finger up to my lips. Even though Juan and Angela are younger than Maria, they stare at me quietly and in another moment, not even Maria fails to recognize the fear in this room.

'Mama,' Maria calls out, and our mother is jarred into action. She hurries across the kitchen and wraps her arms around Maria and Juan. I feel a tinge of jealousy. I wish Mom were holding me right now, even though, at thirteen, I don't feel this way very often.

Quickly I realize that this monster is made of water. It is a liquid beast with water claws and water fangs, with rippling water fur. It is made of rain falling from the sky. I think to myself, why would such a beast

16

choose our little house? Why, of all the little and big houses across all of Honduras would the beast choose us? I'm scared.

I hate being afraid. I am too old to be afraid of rain. But I can't help it. This is so different from any rain I've ever known before.

During the rainy season, we always have storms. So many times, during sudden cloudbursts I've ducked into the house and watched the rain pour down. But there's never been anything like *this* rain before. I hear the monster growling, low and mean. Its voice is the wind roaring all around us. This water isn't like rain at all – there aren't raindrops, but sheets of solid water, like a waterfall crashing down from the sky.

What worries me most is that my father and my brother Victor and my sister Ruby aren't here. Dad usually arrives home before dinnertime. But today he's late and the wind has been so terrible, the storm so awful, that Mom decided not to hold dinner any longer. We'd just sat down to eat when the monster leapt on to our roof. My dad and Victor and Ruby are in Dad's truck. Dad delivers stuff for companies in and around the large city of San Pedro Sula. But they were supposed to be back from a delivery to La Ceiba, a town on the coast seventy miles from here, over an hour ago.

The water monster interrupts my thoughts, shifting its weight; the roof creaks again. The water now drips down into the house, and it is a *lot* of water. On the rainiest, wettest days of past rainy seasons, sometimes our house leaked in two different spots; a place in the kitchen and a place just over the back door. Now, with the monster pressing down upon us so heavily, the house has sprung too many leaks to count – more than a dozen. Mom and Angela and Maria hurry to grab buckets, pots and pans, anything to catch the dripping rain. I can't tell where one leak ends and another begins. The water drips into the house so fast and steady that in some places it looks like it's coming from a faucet.

Mom tells me to grab some black plastic garbage bags and to cover up the entertainment center, the television, VCR and stereo, to keep the water from ruining them. I use duct tape to hold the corners of the bags down snugly. Mom puts plastic over the clothes that hang in our closets, and now we find some large tarps and lay them over our beds to try and keep our blankets from getting too wet.

I hear the monster on our roof laughing at us. His laughter says, 'Forget about saving things – you'll be lucky to save yourselves!' I know that this 'voice' is just in my imagination, but it feels like it's speaking the truth. I shudder at this imaginary voice, then, I quietly swear at myself for my cowardice.

I think about my father again, and Victor and Ruby. Are they all right? When will they get home? I think about my friend, Sandy. She's an American girl whose parents are here in Honduras doing church work. Sandy goes to my school. She's only been in Honduras since August, just a couple of months. I told her about the rainy season, told her how it was fun to hear the slapping of rain on the rooftops. What if Sandy thinks this is normal? I told her the rainy days were fun. Fun? She must think I'm crazy. I wish I could talk to her right now, but when I try to phone her I discover that our telephone isn't working.

Where're my father, brother and sister? How are Sandy and her family? What's going on?

I hear the monster laugh again, his body pressing down. Angela, having run out of containers to catch the dripping rain coming through our roof, flops down on the couch and begins to cry softly, Maria sits cuddling

Juan, and Mom is still trying to catch the water. I think Mom hears the monster laughing, too. In my gut there's a gnawing, like an animal eating at my insides. My chest aches, and my palms are tingly and damp, not from the rain, but from a cold sweat that also covers my forehead and the back of my neck. I've never felt this afraid before.

Two

Even though my sister Maria's little battery-operated radio tells us that this storm has a name – Hurricane Mitch – and even though it's crazy to even try to sleep, Mom sends all of us to bed. I know what she's doing; she wants to pretend that somehow, things are 'normal'. Mom wants to believe that the monster, Hurricane Mitch, isn't really up on our roof, and she wants us to believe that too.

My mother isn't crazy; she's just scared. I see fear in her eyes and in the way her forehead is wrinkled with worry. But in a way, I agree with her – we might as well go to bed. There's nothing helped by sitting up in our dripping house and staring at the ceiling and at each other. I bet that Mom's mostly worried about Dad and Victor and Ruby.

I'm in my bedroom, the one I share with my two brothers. Of course Victor still isn't home. Little Juan has a wide-eyed stare, as he lies silent in his bed. Juan's been quiet ever since the monster leapt on to our house. He's usually a chatter-box, carrying on and on about everything and everyone. Juan watches every music video that comes on and knows all the words. He watches every cartoon in the world and although he's only four years old, he can read the back of cereal boxes and understand what's written there – he speaks the best English of any of us.

Juan's got a collection of plastic action figures that I'm sure rival any collection in the whole country of Honduras. He has all of Victor's old action figures and all of mine too. All told, he must have at least a couple of hundred of these. When he plays with them, they make up a weird group of characters and scenarios. It's not unusual to see Juan playing war games with an antique Teenage Mutant Ninja Turtle and an equally ancient Luke Skywalker. Sometimes, Juan has a baseball player doing mortal combat with Simba from a *Lion King* Happy Meal. He loves to play with these toys in bed at night too, but tonight, in the wet, cold darkness of our room, Juan's quiet.

I ask him, 'Are you afraid, Juan?'

'No,' he answers back, very softly, his voice filled with fear.

I say, 'I'm a little scared.'

'Really?' Juan asks, 'Why?'

'Oh, you know. I hope Dad gets home pretty soon. And this rain and wind is so loud, you know?'

'Yeah,' Juan answers and I can almost hear the wheels turning in his head. 'I won't tell Victor that you're a-scared,' Juan says.

I smile and say, 'Thanks, Juan, you're a good brother.'

We're quiet for a few moments then Juan says, very softly, 'I'm a little bit . . .' He won't let himself actually say the words.

'That's OK,' I reassure him. Then I add, 'I won't tell Victor, either.'

We lay quietly for a while, the room growing darker by the second. Now Juan says, 'Here,' and I hear a 'splat' on the plastic tarp that's covering my blankets.

I reach out and feel around the top of the wet tarp until my fingers find what Juan's thrown to me. It's his C3PO action figure, the gold android from *Star Wars*. Victor had the entire *Star Wars* collection when he was little. Juan lost Princess Leia and threw away Jabba the

Hutt because Jabba was just too scary; otherwise, Juan still has all the pieces. C3PO is his favorite, though.

'Are you sure you want to loan me this?' I ask.

I hear Juan nodding his head in the dark and then I hear him softly say, 'Yes.'

The wind suddenly howls even more loudly and in the gust the rain pounds down. Juan must be really scared.

I say, 'I'll give him back to you first thing in the morning, OK?'

'OK,' Juan answers.

I hear the fear in his voice and I say, 'You can have him back right now if you want. I mean, I know he's one your best ones – you sure you don't want him back?'

Juan considers for a few seconds then says, 'You're kind of a-scared too. You can use him tonight.'

'Thanks Juan,' I say.

'OK,' Juan answers back.

In another few minutes, I hear Juan snoring softly, just like he snores every night. His snores sound funny, so tiny and weak. If it weren't so wet in our room, if the floor wasn't covered with water, I'd get up and put C3PO back in Juan's bed with him. But I don't want to get my feet all wet and I don't want to risk waking up Juan either. Talking to Juan, reassuring him, helped me forget about my own fear for a few minutes, but now I feel it shifting around inside me again. My skin feels so damp and there is a kind of coldness inside me, like the rain is sneaking into me somehow – I can't explain it, really. I just know I feel afraid.

As I think this thought, the monster pounds on the roof again. The house creaks terribly, moans under the monster's movement. I lie very still and try to empty my fear from my mind and heart. For three hours now this monster of water has been pressing down upon us. How long can he stay here? I need to get some sleep.

I don't know when exactly I finally doze off. Maybe some of the time I'm asleep, dreaming I'm still awake. But finally I do have a dream that I know, even while it's happening, is a dream. It's Christmas time in La Rupa – a typical Honduran Christmas day. Never do five seconds pass without the sound of firecrackers popping. Sparkling bottle rockets and whirling flames light up the daytime sky. The blue smoke and the sulfur smell of gunpowder fill the air. I'm so excited; I feel like I might explode with happiness. This Christmas Day is just like every Christmas I've ever known. The smells, the sights, the warm feeling on my skin – everything is perfect, wonderful.

But as my dream goes on, it's not Christmas anymore. It's just a regular old day in La Rupa: Mr and Mrs Barabon sit on their porch, Mr and Mrs Cortez walk along the street, it seems that all of La Rupa's children are running around playing. The Arroyos are in their little store. Vera Ramerez smiles at me and waves; the steep, green hills rise all around us – the hills seem to breathe; their breath is the air we breathe, warm and safe. It's quiet, except for the occasional barking of a dog and the soft breeze, blowing sweetly across the town.

Suddenly, I am in our house. Mom and my two younger sisters, Maria and Angela, stand together in the kitchen. Mom is smiling and talking to Maria, who laughs through her wide smile; Angela's dark eyes are laughing too. Again, happiness fills me; I want to laugh out loud. And now, as I look out the window, I see a flock of beautiful wild parrots fly across our backyard, their black eyes staring in at us – but their stares feel strange to me, like they are trying to warn me of some danger.

Now it's Christmas again, but the warm feeling is gone. Something's wrong. I'm opening a present only it's wrapped up too tightly. I tug and pick away at the wrapper, but I don't seem to be getting anywhere. Then I hear a terrible, low growling sound. I look up from the gift I've been trying to unwrap. The growl is too deep and scary to be a dog, even a large dog. The growl slowly turns into a soft, terrible howl. I feel scared, but I don't want to show it. Somehow I realize that by acting brave I will be all right. The gift in my hand turns into a large, gray stone, too big to throw, but still a comfort, a weapon I can use to fight off whatever is howling just outside the walls.

Suddenly I realize a terrible fact, I can't find my little brother Juan. Why isn't he here? I *am* dreaming, aren't I? But shouldn't he be here in the room with me? Where is my house? Where is my town? Where is everyone? Where's Juan?! I can barely catch a breath. My chest heaves and aches, my stomach feels like lead and my hands shake from fear.

I wake up to a huge puddle of cold water on the tarp right over my lap. For a half a second I'm embarrassed, it looks like I've wet the bed. But in another moment

I'm awake and I hear the monster all around me. I hear it laughing at my fear. I look over at Juan's bed where he's awake too. Remembering my dream, I'm thankful that at least the monster hasn't hurt him.

The rain has stopped while we've been sleeping. This is good; I was starting to worry that the monster had swallowed the sun. But maybe later this morning, when I wake up again, the sun will be back and everything will be normal. Maybe the family of wild parrots that lives behind our house, on the steep hillside rising up along the north of La Rupa, will come back again. Of course, you wouldn't expect to see them when the rain is falling so hard, but since it's stopped, maybe they'll come back?

Juan asks, 'Do you think it will rain again?'

I answer, 'Yes, I'm afraid it probably will, maybe not so heavy though, and maybe not for so long.'

The wind's still blowing hard, but without the rain it doesn't feel so threatening.

Juan says, 'I bet Victor is mad at the rain.'

'Oh yeah,' I agree, 'Victor is probably telling the rain what will happen if it keeps falling down.'

'Yeah,' Juan says, 'Victor will kill the rain if it keeps falling.'

I smile and answer, 'He will, Juan, he'll kick the rain's butt!'

Juan loves to hear Victor and I use expressions like this. He never repeats them himself though, Juan even says, 'Oh my Goll,' instead of 'Oh my God.'

'I bet Ruby's sad that she hasn't seen me,' Juan says.

'Oh yes,' I answer, 'I'm sure she misses you. But she'll be home soon and then she'll give you a big hug.'

'No way!' Juan says, wrinkling his nose.

I smile; Juan wouldn't want Victor to see him enjoying a hug from Ruby. Victor would call him 'Baby-J', a nickname Juan hates.

Juan's quiet a few moments then asks softly, 'They are coming back, huh?' his voice very tiny, 'They love us, even when we're bad and so they will come home, right?'

I wonder what Juan means, the thing about seeing Ruby and about being bad? It's almost like he thinks he's being punished for something. Could Juan think that Dad and Victor and Ruby are gone because of him, because of some bad thing he thinks he did or thought? Little kids are so weird.

I speak to him softly. 'The storm has kept them away, Juan. It's not *your* fault. This storm is terrible and it comes from the sky and it has nothing to do with us, with how good or bad we are – *everybody* is getting wet and is tired and hurt by this storm, good guys and bad guys both. It's not your fault. It's nobody's fault. Dad and Victor and Ruby will be back when the storm lets them. This storm's a monster that doesn't care about us, but it *will* go away someday.'

Juan says, 'Yes,' softly. I can hear the sleepiness in his voice and sure enough, within a few minutes I hear his little snoring.

I lie in the darkness thinking about what I've just said to Juan. This storm *is* a monster. How long can it last? Will it ever end?

Before I go to sleep again, the rain comes back. But it's not like the rain from earlier, not so heavy. In fact, our roof is holding out most of the water and the sound of the rain falling is almost pleasant, reminding me of how the rain is supposed to be. The winds have calmed down too. I feel a sense of safety for the first time all night. My hands are steady and my insides are calm. My breathing feels almost relaxed. Maybe the storm is going away? I drift into sleep, my eyes and body and soul tired but hopeful.

★ ★ ★

I dream that I'm flying over Honduras, only it doesn't look like Honduras. There are bright lights, like fireflies, only brighter. Soon, I recognize the lights as coming from the little houses of La Rupa down below me. I'm high up in the sky. Two wild parrots are flying next to me. One of them is so close that I can look at his eye; it is bright and shiny and looks right back at me.

I am happy in my dream. It feels good to be so free.

Suddenly there is a tremendous explosion, like the world is cracking in two. All the dream lights below me go out and I can't tell if I am flying or falling in the darkness. The wild parrots disappear.

Now I'm in that strange place between dreaming and waking up, and I hear a strange, distant sound of crying and moaning. The earth quivers under my bed; I feel it shaking. What is this?

Juan cries out to me, 'Jose!'

I'm awake. I jump out of my bed, grabbing Juan up into my arms.

In the darkness, just waking up from my dream, I still feel confused. The house seems to shake all around me. Is it really shaking or is it just my legs? Is this all real? Is *any* of it real?

Before I can get my bearings there is another huge *'THUMP!'* This one, truly, shakes the whole world. I almost fall down as the shock wave hits me, and now I know that it's not just me, not just my legs; my sleepiness has nothing to do with this explosion, it's like a bomb went off. *What's happening?*

I stumble into the living room, with Juan in my arms. Mom and the girls are here too. We have all managed to find one another.

Mom asks, panic in her voice, 'What is it?'

I answer, 'I don't know, Mom.'

Angela says, 'The world is breaking apart!'

'What?' Maria says at first, then she agrees with her, 'Yes, broken! Broken!'

The girls' fears, once again, pull Mom out of herself. 'No,' Mom says, her voice calming us down.

Even in the darkness, even though we can't see anything, I suddenly realize what's happening. Earlier tonight, the radio told about mudslides across Northern Honduras. I think the hillside behind La Rupa has let loose. The monster has reached up, sweeping his clawed hand and torn away part of La Rupa's flesh.

I say, 'It's a mudslide!'

Mom asks us, 'Is anyone hurt?'

In the darkness, Juan, dressed in *X Files* underpants and a white T-shirt, shakes his head 'no' to Mom's question. I answer, 'Juan and I are fine.'

Now, voices from outside are calling out for help, growing louder and louder. Juan asks, 'Is that Dad and Ruby?'

'No,' I tell him as I hand him to Mom. 'It's our friends, it's La Rupa.'

I hurry back to my room and pull on my pants and a T-shirt. I grab my jacket and slip into my Nike high-tops.

By the time I come out of my bedroom, Mom is standing at the front door with a flashlight. She hands it to me and says, 'Be careful!'

I look into her eyes and see her fear. She hasn't said that she doesn't want me to go out. Of course, neither of us *wants* me to go, but we know that I have to.

Mom's fear grabs the inside of me too. My hands shake and my stomach flip-flops. Sweat breaks out on my forehead and I can feel it running down my sides, under my arms. For a second, I just stand there frozen with fear.

Mom says again, 'Be careful, Jose!'

Her words snap me out of it. 'I will be Mom, I promise!'

I open the door, pull my collar up against the rain, and step outside.

Three

It's so dark as I move off the porch. My flashlight seems useless, a tiny dot of light trying to move over everything – it doesn't even reach the houses across the street, much less down the street. I stand here for a moment and keep passing the dot of light all around the town; I don't see anything.

I hear people crying out and start to move towards their voices, but within a few steps I suddenly sink into mud up to my knees. I keep waving my flashlight so that the people calling might see and help me find them.

This stupid light is worthless! Where are all the houses? Where are— And now it hits me. The light won't shine on the houses, because—

The Ramerez house, which used to stand right next door to ours, is *gone*. So, too, are the Alverez house and the Larios' house. Where are they? How do you make a whole house just . . . *disappear*?

I force myself to look out into the darkness, squinting as hard as I can to look for all the other houses, which I can normally see from our front porch. I can't see anything.

I don't know what time it is, but it must be nearly sunrise. With each second that passes, I can see further and further down the street. I wish I couldn't.

Far on the other side of the village it looks like there is a fire, flames rise up for a few moments and then, as if by some kind of magic, the flames go instantly black. Do I imagine this?

Am I imagining all of this? I mean this can't be real, can it? If all the houses are just *gone*, where are all the people? If all the houses have been swept away by the mudslide, where are the people who were sleeping in those houses?

Where *is* everybody?

The rain falls in a slow, steady drizzle. If this had happened earlier, when it was raining so hard, it would have been even worse. Worse? I look at the devastation and see that La Rupa is gone! What could be 'worse' than 'gone'?

I hear moans coming from where the Ramerez house used to be. I struggle over, slogging through a knee-deep river of mud. The roof has been torn off their house; it lies in the street, flattened out. All the roof trusses are broken and crushed. The walls of the house are still standing, but only the tops of those walls stick out of the mud. And the mud is everywhere, brown, wet, and thick; it looks like the filthy fur of an animal.

Suddenly I see Mr Ramerez. He is sticking up out of the ground; but it's only the upper half of him, only his upper body. His hair, normally a thinning salt and pepper color, looks brown, like the mud that covers him. His eyes dart all over as he whips his head back and forth.

None of this feels real. Am I still in a nightmare? I look down and can't see my feet; the mud is up high over my ankles. How many times have I kicked a soccer ball on this street? What street? How many times have I run past the Ramerez house, the Alverez house, all the houses, heading home after school? What houses? Where is the street? How could the monster just grab a whole house, a whole town and make it disappear? Where is La Rupa? I begin to shake all over as I struggle through the mud – I'm scared, afraid to move, afraid not to . . .

Mr Ramerez's cries grab me. At first I can't make out what he's saying but then I hear more clearly, 'Vera!' he calls over and over again. For some reason I think about Vera Ramerez and my mom baking pies together every autumn. I look around for Vera, but I don't see her anyplace. Now it strikes me. Is she buried in the mud?

'Vera!' Mr Ramerez calls, again and again.

I call back to Mr Ramerez, 'I don't see her! Have you seen her since the mud hit your house?'

'Vera?' Mr Ramerez calls to me.

'No, Mr Ramerez, it's me, Jose Cruz.'

'Where is Vera?' he asks.

'I don't see her,' I answer, struggling to make my way over to him.

I ask him, 'Can you move your legs, are you hurt?'

Mr Ramerez says, 'Don't worry about me, find Vera!'

I say, 'I don't know where she is, Mr Ramerez, I don't see her anywhere. Let me help you first, then we can look for her together.'

'Yes. Good, Jose. Yes.' He looks up at my face as I get closer. His eyes are scared.

I finally make it over to him. I reach under his arms and across his chest, locking my hands; his body feels cold. Once I have him in a strong grip, I begin to tug him up. At first, I sink in deeper and I feel a rush of fear; is the mud going to swallow both of us? But in another few seconds Mr Ramerez begins to break loose and we're both lifted, as if invisible hands are pushing us up.

Just as Mr Ramerez is breaking free, Carlos and Pablo Altunez call to us from where the street used to be. They're fighting their way through the mud towards us. The sky is light now, and I see more of the damage.

My first impression was right. There is no more La Rupa. Only two houses still stand, our place and, way across town, the tiny shack of the Rodriquez family. These two places, the Rodriquez's and ours, are far apart – our house is in the northwest corner of La Rupa and the Rodriquez place is in the southeast. Everything in between these two structures is twisted and broken or completely gone.

Parts of houses still stand, but they lean at terrible angles, held up only by the mud packed around them, three and four and five feet deep. All that's left of most of the houses are broken rooftops lying on the ground.

Carlos and Pablo call out to us, 'Help! Can you help us?'

Carlos says, 'Our parents are buried, help us, please!'

Pablo begins to cry.

'Vera is lost,' Mr Ramerez says. 'Vera! Vera!' he calls out.

Pablo, crying harder, begins to moan, 'Oh God, oh God.'

I say to them, 'Go back to your house and dig, hurry! Use a shovel if you can find one, or a stick, or your bare hands if you have to – maybe your parents are still alive. Go and dig them out!'

Where does my certainty come from? It's as though I'm standing outside myself, watching myself give orders. I realize that I'm acting like Victor would act if he were here. Victor's always so sure of himself, always so certain that whatever he decides is the right thing. Somehow I'm being guided by Victor, by a sense of his strength and will.

Carlos and Pablo Altunez hurry away from us, back towards the place where their home used to be, moving as fast as the terrible mud will let them.

Mr Ramerez begins to dig, calling out, 'Vera! Vera!' over and over.

I help him for a few minutes, but then I hear the groans of other people, who need help too. I leave Mr Ramerez, making my way towards the other voices; he doesn't even notice my leaving.

I move through La Rupa, towards the broken, leaning houses, past the rooftops lying on the mud. How many of my neighbors are still alive? Will I be able to help anyone? I don't know which way to turn; so many people are calling for help. Where is Victor? Where's my father? They'd know what to do. My eyes start to burn, but I choke off the tears, take a few deep breaths.

I force myself along what used to be the main street of town, now it's just a river of mud; I'm tired and cold and aching, my hands hurt and my legs and feet feel like they're being scraped raw with sandpaper, but I force myself to keep going. I have to try to help, but the storm doesn't care, it roars on.

Four

I sit on the tile floor of our living room, too tired to stand up.

Vera Ramerez is dead. Mr Ramerez found her body after an hour of digging down into the wet earth. Mr Ramerez seems to be in shock. They have no children. Vera was his whole family. He sits on a mud-splattered chair in front of where his house used to be and his mouth is twisted tightly, his eyes dark and red; he looks sad and confused.

The best we can figure so far is that thirty-two more people died in the mudslide, Vera Ramerez and thirty-two more. Thirty-three people from our town of fifty-six – it feels like we all have died. I remember the faces of the people who are gone now, of course Mrs Ramerez, but so many others, Allegra Barabon with her hair in pig-tails, Raul Ortega kicking a soccer ball, the entire Baronas family – their smiles and eyes and their voices. But every time I think of them, my eyes start to get tears and sting, so I force myself to think of other things. My body aches; my legs and arms feel weak. I won't let myself cry, but I'm so tired, so worn out.

Before last night, there were twelve houses in La Rupa and it was pretty much my whole world. Before last night, there were twelve families living in those houses. I guess we were just like lots of other small Honduran towns – quiet, easy-going, maybe a little lazy, but safe and comfortable. Most of all, this place was home. Now we are . . . nothing. Now we are . . . gone!

Maria's radio tells us that all over Honduras it's just like here in La Rupa. Somehow this news doesn't help, doesn't make our losses any easier to take.

My friend Alfredo Menendoz walks into town, and up to our house. Alfredo lives with his family outside of La Rupa. Thinking about all our lost homes and people here, I didn't remember the Menendoz. Alfredo says that they are all OK.

Alfredo is my age, thirteen, and we've played sports in school competitions ever since we were little kids.

'Where—' begins Alfredo, hesitating and pausing, 'What happened to all the houses?'

Maria, who is standing beside Mom, says, 'The mud slid them away.'

'Mudslide,' I say.

'Yes,' Alfredo answers and then he's silent.

Like me, Alfredo is also a student at a private, bilingual school in San Pedro Sula, the International Sanpedrono. So now he speaks to me in English.

'What are you to do to these too many people?' he asks. His grammar is wrong, but I get his meaning. A dozen of our neighbors are crowded into our little house, some of them hurt, some of them so tired and lost in grief that we can't tell if they are injured or not. Alfredo is speaking English because he doesn't want these people to hear him asking how we plan to deal with them.

I answer in English, 'I don't know, Alfredo. The only other house still standing is the Rodriquez place and it's too small. They have already taken in people too. They have ten people there.'

Neither Alfredo nor I have to say out loud what we are both thinking; it would be *impossible* for ten people to even fit into the Rodriquez place, built of lumber scraps, palm fronds and pieces of plastic. There is only one room to their whole house and in that room the mother, father and three children live.

'Ten people?' Alfredo says, still speaking English, 'Amazing.'

I say, 'Yes,' and nod.

A few of the people in our house, those sitting and lying down on the floor listening to Alfredo and I talking, are starting to look nervous. They probably wonder why we're speaking in English, what we're hiding from them.

I shift our conversation back to Spanish so that everyone will know what we're saying. 'We will help everyone we can for as long as we can. My father and older brother and sister are missing, we haven't heard from them since the storm started.'

As Alfredo nods his understanding, I realize that I have called my father and brother and sister 'missing'. The radio has told us that thousands of people are 'missing'. A sick feeling rises inside my chest and through my stomach. I correct myself.

'Not *missing*,' I say, 'but we haven't heard from them yet.'

'I understand,' Alfredo says.

There's an uncomfortable silence between us — my stomach comes up further into my throat; I taste the acid.

Forcing myself not to be sick, I ask Alfredo, 'Can you take in some people at your house to help out?'

Alfredo looks around at everyone packed into our living room. Some of them look up at him and some of them intentionally look away.

'I'll ask my mother,' Alfredo answers.

'Good,' I say.

After another few moments, Alfredo leaves, promising that he'll be back before night falls.

I should never have said the thing about, 'What could be worse than gone?' La Rupa is *people* more than buildings and yards and streets. Since some of us are still alive, La Rupa is still alive . . . But it's not the same, and I don't know what to call it.

What do you call a place that's still here but isn't really? What's the name for a place that yesterday was home to neighbors and houses and wild parrots and kids on Big Wheel bikes, but that's now . . . not *gone*, but . . . I don't know how to say it.

La Rupa is like a ghost . . . not a ghost, exactly, but if I close my eyes I can still see the town exactly like it was. If I close my eyes really tight then open them real fast and close them again, I can still see, for just a second all the houses still here, all the people still alive . . .

And there *are* still three real houses: ours, the Rodriquez's and, over the hillside, the Menendoz place. And there are all my friends and neighbors, sitting on our floor and furniture, many wearing pajamas and barefoot, coated or splattered in mud. They sit staring at the floor or into space, silent, like ghosts too. La Rupa isn't gone, it's just . . . I don't know what to say.

But I *do* know that La Rupa *has* to survive because if it dies my dad and brother and sister won't have anyplace to come back to. Thinking this, my stomach shifts sickeningly again, my chest aches and my heart races.

Five

I go to the back door of our house. I push it back and forth, moving the mud to force the door open. I'm careful not to break the door loose from its hinges; it takes several minutes to get it open far enough so that I can squeeze out. I don't understand why the mud didn't bury our house too.

We're at the far edge of town, but unlike the Rodriquez house, which just happened to be a few feet away from where the mud flowed, our house is surrounded by tree branches, water, and sloppy muck that was once the hillside behind us. What destroyed all the other houses should have taken us down too. Why were we spared? Once I'm out the back door, I know the answer. Victor's barbecue, Victor's Folly.

Jammed up against the backside of the huge brick

barbecue, is an enormous boulder, almost five feet tall. It must weigh tons. The bottom half of this boulder is covered in mud, but the top half, standing almost as tall as the barbecue, has been washed clean by the rain. The rock is blackish gray, its surface covered by cracks and ledges, craggy and sharp.

I see what happened. When the hillside gave way, this huge boulder came with it. I think back to being woken by the mudslide; first, the hillside collapsed, trees, topsoil and the earth coming down. I heard the debris sliding into, through, and over the town. But next came that second, big shock wave, and that was this huge boulder slamming into the barbecue. Our whole house quivered and I almost fell down.

I look at the boulder more closely, touching its surface. If it wasn't for Victor's barbecue, this rock would have come straight through our house. We would have been crushed.

Instead this huge rock pushed up against Victor's brick barbecue, and when the mud hit this blockade, it went around us, just clipping the back corners of our house with too little force to do any damage. Thinking about this, I realize that my hands are quivering, not from cold but from the horror at what might have happened. I can barely catch my breath thinking of how bad it could have been.

Victor's barbecue saved us. Victor's Folly has given our neighbors a safe, dry place to eat and sleep and take shelter. I think about Victor again, about him being gone with Dad and Ruby; God, I hope they're all right. Please God, let my dad and Victor and Ruby be all right.

I wander over to the corner of our backyard, mud covering my feet to my ankles as I walk. I glance at what used to be La Rupa. For the first time since this all started, because no one is nearby, I cry hard, letting everything out. Sobs wrench my body. My chest hurts, and my ribs ache from crying so hard. My stomach retches over and over; my throat burns. Sweat breaks out on my face and under my arms. My nose runs like a faucet. I cry and cry and as bad as it feels, it also feels good; it feels right to cry like this.

Weird thoughts race through my brain. All my life, as the second son, I've struggled to hold my own, afraid of being weak, or of letting down my guard. As I weep now, I feel different. I'm not ashamed, not embarrassed. Tears stream down my cheeks and find their way into my mouth. These tears have a gritty taste to them – I think to myself, crunchy tears. In another moment, I am laughing and crying at the same time. Finally, I can't cry any more. There is too much to do to indulge my emotions any longer, anyway.

If La Rupa is going to survive, it's going to need help – feelings, wants and wishes aren't important right now. I've spent my whole life looking up to Victor and my dad, but they aren't here. I've always wondered what's really inside me: how much courage? How much cowardice? I didn't invite this disaster, and I'm horrified by it. And yet *because* of it, I have to be strong for the first time. Dad and Victor can't help. It's up to me, now. I wipe my arm across my nose and rub the heels of my hands in my eyes to get rid of the last of my tears. I steady my breathing, and talk to myself, Take it easy, I say, Slow and easy. My stomach quiets down. There's no time now for tears or laughter. There is only time for surviving.

Six

It's the second day of the storm, morning. Even though all the phone lines are messed up, somehow our phone service is partially working. This seems crazy, but you can see the wires still attached to the poles, although the poles lie on the ground. Trying to reach the outside world, I dial every number I can think of and I finally get through to my American friend Sandy.

'You're alive!' she cries out. Her voice is scratchy over the line. Although the phone works, I'm worried we'll lose our connection. I can't believe how warm and good I feel just hearing her voice.

We're speaking English and I'm self-conscious. When I'm at school or when I'm with Sandy, my English is actually pretty good. Having a native English-speaking friend (a really *pretty* native English-speaking friend) has been a big help in learning the language. But now, between my feelings and all that's happened these last few days, I have to struggle to find the right words.

'Yes, I'm alive,' I say back.

Sandy starts to cry.

'Don't cry,' I joke, 'maybe we'll get lucky and the next mudslide will kill me too.'

This attempt at humor doesn't go over too well; Sandy cries even harder.

'That was a joke,' I say, 'I'm fine, really, I'm OK.'

'Is your family all right?' Sandy asks through her tears.

I think about telling her about Dad and Victor and Ruby, but I don't want her to cry anymore and I can't even think of how to explain it in English. For days now, except for that one short talk with Alfredo, I've been speaking nothing but Spanish. I have to concentrate so hard for even this simple conversation.

I answer her, 'We're OK for now.' Not exactly a lie – I hope all of us *are* OK – I've been praying for that.

'We're leaving,' Sandy says.

'Where are you going?' I ask.

'Home,' Sandy answers.

I'm confused for a moment. Home? If she hasn't

been staying in her home in San Pedro Sula, where has she been?

'Home?' I ask.

'The States.'

For some reason, my mind chooses this moment to go blank of everything except Sandy's looks: I think about her long, blonde hair, her cute feet with their long, skinny toes, her slender hands, her smile and the color of her blue eyes.

'*Que?*' (What?) I ask in Spanish, forgetting to use even that simple English word.

'Back home to the States,' Sandy says again.

'Sure,' I say, coming back to reality. 'Home,' I say absently.

Sandy's family has a house in Minnesota. I think it's near Canada. Sandy is an only child. Her parents came to Honduras as part of a mission for their church. My thoughts tumble over each other in English words: Canada . . . mud . . . 'blonde . . . God.' Suddenly I feel weird, really frustrated.

'I don't want to go,' Sandy begins, but then changes this. 'What I mean is, that I don't want to leave you or my other friends or the school – but it *is* terrible here now.'

She talks about not having any hot water for a shower, about not having any electricity, about being worried that they will run out of bottled water.

Sandy says, 'Everything is just so inconvenient.'

I feel my face start to burn and I almost blurt out, 'Yes, I understand, my whole town has been *destroyed*; friends are *dead* under tons of mud; it certainly is *inconvenient*, isn't it?'

But even in my anger, I check the urge to say these things. Still, this conversation feels bad; my hand feels weak and shaky even holding the phone.

'Is it terrible in La Rupa?' she asks.

'Yes, it's really bad – too terrible to talk about.' For just a second I consider telling her the whole truth. Instead I ask, 'When will you be leaving?'

It hurts to ask even this; I wish I could spit the words out, and the feelings that go with them.

Sandy says, 'The airport at San Pedro Sula is under three feet of water. The military airport at Xalopa is the only one in the country that still works. My dad thinks we can get out on a plane tomorrow morning.'

'*Manana*?' I ask, slipping back into Spanish, unable to keep the surprise and disappointment out of my voice.

Her words 'get out' echo through my mind: *get out . . . get out . . . get out.*

'I know,' Sandy says, her voice filling with sadness again, 'We won't even have a chance to say goodbye.'

Putting the best thoughts I can on this, I say, 'We'll write to each other. And later, maybe you'll come back to visit.' I don't know what else to say. My brain keeps flipping around. My feelings are scrambled. For a few seconds, I remember when Sandy and I met and first became friends. We went swimming and playing at the beach out in Tela. The blue waters of the Caribbean were the same color as her eyes. That was the first time I saw her in a bathing suit – she had the palest skin; I was surprised at how white, almost pure white, her flesh looked. Of course, I made sure not to let her catch me staring at her breasts in her bikini top, which looked almost blue they were so pale – but I remember the colors of our bodies as we sat next to each other, mine so dark and brown, and hers so white.

'I'll miss you,' Sandy says, interrupting my memories. She begins to cry again.

'I'll miss you too,' I say and even though I mean it, even though I like Sandy a lot, I am so distracted by so many other feelings that I feel almost dishonest saying it. I feel like she's already gone – like, maybe, she was never *really* here at all . . .

I say, 'Write me, with your new address,' trying not to sound too hurried, but wanting to get off the phone.

'I will, I promise,' Sandy says then she adds 'Good luck' in Spanish, '*Buenos suerte.*'

'Thanks, you too,' I say, then, almost too quickly, 'Goodbye.'

'Bye Jose,' Sandy says and starts to say, 'I'll miss y—'

I hang up.

I think about Sandy, 'Going home,' 'Getting out'. And the more I think about it, the angrier I become.

I'm mad that Sandy's family can just 'get out', but I'm happy for them too. Why should they leave? Why shouldn't they? This isn't their home, or they couldn't, *wouldn't*, just 'get out'. I'm confused, big time.

I walk out the front door of our house and stand on the top of the three cement steps that lead down to the sidewalk and street. I look at what used to be La Rupa; there is *so* much to do, too much to do – people's lives to save, a whole world to save! I feel a sudden burst of energy; my heart pounds in my chest.

Seven

'I know this sounds terrible and I'm so sorry to have to say it, but we must leave the rest of the bodies where they are,' Mr Cortez is speaking, tears nearly choking off his words. All day yesterday and all day today, for two days now the men of La Rupa and we older boys, have dug and scraped at the earth searching for our relatives and friends. Using shovels and rakes, sticks and our bare hands, we've clawed our way into the mud hoping and praying we might find more survivors. Our hands are bloody with blisters, cuts and scratches. My back aches from so much digging. But we found no one alive, only the dead bodies of two children, Allegra Barabon, the little girl with pig-tails who teased me when Victor and I were building the barbecue, and her little brother Edgar, and one adult, Maria Handel.

58

Now, in our living room, a dozen people sit crammed together, trying to decide what to do about friends and loved ones that still lie buried. Everybody agrees that by now, two days and nights after the mudslide, only the dead are left under the stinking, brackish mud.

Suddenly Mr Ramerez mumbles, 'I pulled my Vera from the mud and now she is wrapped in plastic, under stones in the yard.' He pauses, staring off into space. Dirt still covers his hands and is packed under his nails. His fingers are cut and torn from using his bare hands to dig. He seems so different, not like the same man who, a week ago, tossed a soccer ball back to us after it had landed in his yard, not like the same man who, a few months ago, teased Victor about our barbecue being a jailhouse.

Mr Cortez gazes at Mr Ramerez sadly, then looks around the room at all of us. 'Perhaps later we will be able to bring everyone up from the mud. Maybe when we get help. But right now we have no coffins, we have no place to put the bodies – and we can't help those who are already gone.'

There's silence in the room, but we all nod. We're like zombies. I barely recognize some of these people that I've seen every day of my life – they're like stunned, muddy strangers. But maybe everybody's also quiet because we all know that for the moment at least, we should try to agree about things. We don't know how long it will be until help arrives. And who will that help be? If all of Honduras is as bad as La Rupa, who can come here and when? What if no help comes at all? One thing I'm sure of, our survival depends on working together. If even *I* understand this, I'm sure all the adults must get it too. Looking at my friends and neighbors, I feel proud of us all.

The storm continues throughout the afternoon, but now it's almost an afterthought. None of us pays much attention to the monster. Maybe if we ignore him long enough Hurricane Mitch will just get tired of us and leave us alone. The wind's still terrible and the rain still falls, at times very heavily, at times in cold drizzle. But what can Mitch do to us now? What more can he take? The wind blows and the rain falls but we sit quietly, calmly, just waiting for it to pass.

Mom brings in two large pots, one of beans and one of rice and sets them on the table in the kitchen. There's no tap water to wash the dishes, but nobody complains about having to use a slightly greasy plate or forks or spoons. Nobody pushes or shoves. Nobody asks for more than their share, or argues or complains about the portions they're served. Everyone just says, 'Thank you' or 'God bless.'

As I'm finishing my meal, Mom calls to me, and signals, with a tilt of her head, for me to follow. I set my plate down and go with her.

We walk to the back of the house.

I've cleared enough mud away from the back door so that it now opens and closes easily. Although there's still a mountain of mud in our yard, I've also shoveled out the space in front of the barbecue so that Mom's able to cook. Our stack of firewood is wet, but with enough old newspaper we got a fire going. As I walk out the door, I look again at the huge boulder, leaning against the barbecue. It looks ridiculous, that boulder and Victor's barbecue give Mom the largest and heaviest cooking apparatus in the history of the world.

Standing in front of the grill, Mom shuts the door behind us. I glance at her and see the concern in her eyes. I'm surprised to see Mom look like this; she's been so strong. Her fear makes me afraid too. A jolt of adrenaline makes my muscles twitch.

'Look,' Mom says, opening the black plastic garbage bags, which hold our supplies of beans and rice.

I'm shocked by how little is left. For half a second I feel dizzy and confused, also angry. How can there be so little food? 'Did someone steal?' I ask.

'No Jose, of course not. There are just so many.'

I take a deep breath again. Of course, Mom's right. She's cooked servings for seventeen people, the five of us and a dozen of our neighbors for several days now. I feel ashamed that I suspected anybody of stealing, but Mom's next words jar me.

'We have to find more food, fast!' she says.

'Yes,' I answer, but I think, more food? Where? All the houses are buried in mud or gone.

Trying to keep the worry out of my voice, I ask, 'Where will we find food?'

'Maybe the Arroyos?' my mother says gently.

Of course, the Arroyos little grocery!

The Arroyos' little store, their *trucha*, had lots of canned goods – milk, beans, baby food, fruit, vegetables, meat, tuna, lots of stuff. But the Arroyos house is gone. All of the food is buried. How can we get it?

Mom reads my mind, 'You'll have to dig.'

'Yes,' I answer.

Eight

The first thing this morning, the third day after the mudslide, two of the men who are staying at our house, Mr Larios and Mr Barabon, and one of the boys, Jorge Alverez, come with me to excavate the foul mud where the Arroyos' place used to be.

Because it's stopped raining for the last hour or so, the mud has begun to dry out. By taking gentle steps, we can actually walk without sinking down very far. It doesn't take long for us to reach the Arroyos.

As we stand staring at the dark muck, where the house used to be, I say to the others, 'The store was here, I think, but the mud has moved everything back. Look at their roof.' The broken, splintered lumber and metal roofing is scattered on the ground, twenty-five to thirty feet back from the street, as if the monster had simply grabbed it and flicked it away. I feel sick as I speak. If I were to burp right now, I'd throw up. But I control the tone of my voice and my words, trying to sound calm and sensible. 'I think that the mud pushed *everything* back, so we should start digging about here.'

I point to a spot ten feet or so from the street and where we're standing; this is where I'm guessing the little store part of the house used to be. My workmates nod and we begin digging.

It's hard work. The mud is sloppy and foul. Each shovelful seems heavier than the last. The blisters on my hands from digging before, looking for survivors, quickly tear open and start to bleed, but I don't complain, nor do I stop working even for a second. After all, it was my idea to dig here, what if we're not even close to where the food is buried? What if—

My thoughts are interrupted as I pull up a shovelful of wet mud and am greeted by a human hand, fingers outstretched as though it is reaching towards me.

Nine

Edgar and Alicia Arroyos' three children are all grown-up and moved away years ago, so I'm sure that the only bodies down here are Edgar and Alicia's. It will take awhile to get all the mud moved away from them. I'm careful not to let the blade of my shovel dig into them; each of us, as we dig, is careful. When the bodies of Allegra and Edgar Barabon and of Mrs Handel were found yesterday, I wasn't digging there, I was with another group at a different spot, so Mr and Mrs Arroyos are the first dead people I have seen.

The closer we come to getting them out, the more a terrible stench overpowers us. I fight back gagging, but my eyes water and my throat stings. Mr Barabon and Mr Larios look as uncomfortable as I am. Jorge Alverez steps away and sits down, retching every few moments and spitting to clear the bile from his mouth. I try to think about things other than the smell.

It looks like when the mud covered them, the Arroyos were still in their bed. They never knew what hit them, except maybe in the final seconds when Mr Arroyos reached up. They lie curled up, in sleeping positions, facing away from each other. It looks almost as though they are still asleep, two slumbering neighbors, resting peacefully under a ton of mud. If it weren't for the smell I might even believe that I could still shake them awake.

After close to an hour of careful digging, we lift their mud-encrusted bodies out and lay them carefully down.

I don't want to look at the Arroyos too closely, but I can't stop myself. Their hands, bare feet, their faces and bodies don't look human anymore — I mean, of course they look a little like they used to, but with the life gone from their bodies, they're not themselves any longer. They look like wax sculptures.

The skin on Mrs Arroyos' hand is flaking off, not sunburn flaking, but peeling away, like rotting fruit or like the scales of a snake.

I remember buying treats from Mrs Arroyos, taking sticks of peppermint and strawberry candy from that hand. I remember Mr Arroyos sweeping in front of the little store, and lifting the grated screen over the open window first thing in the morning, turning and waving to us as we walked past him. Now, dead, even if they weren't caked in mud, they'd still look like strangers. I think about ghosts. I think about dead animals I've seen on the roads and the way that tiny flies and red ants swarm over a rotting mango. It's scary. Death is real. I wonder if it sees me here and thinks about me? A shiver runs down my spine, then back up again.

We lay a black plastic tarp over the Arroyos' bodies, and then we go back to digging for food. I can't stop thinking about how horrible the Arroyos look, and I try hard not to look at the black plastic that covers them.

Death is mean; it doesn't care what you're doing, or how you look, or what people will think of you when they find your lifeless body. Death just takes everything away and leaves a shell behind for your neighbors to dig out of the mud. I feel death staring at me; silent for now, but staring and waiting.

As we work, once in awhile I glance over at Mr and Mrs Arroyos lying under the black plastic. They're still facing away from each other in death like they were in bed the last night of their lives. I think about my dad, about when he'll come home and cuddle close with my mom in their bed again. Normally, I'd never think about my mom and dad in bed, but it's nicer than thinking about death!

Finally we find the first of the food, two filthy cans of corn and another of green beans. With even this small start, I feel more hopeful. We keep digging. And soon, it's like finding treasure.

The Arroyos' little store is a godsend. We find soggy cardboard box after soggy cardboard box full of canned foods. All of the things I'd remembered seeing on their shelves before, and so much more: canned hams, peaches, pears, Jolly Green Giant vegetables, creamed corn, soups of every type: canned chili, meat, and fruit.

But our most amazing find is the huge containers that the Arroyos used to store rice, beans and flour. Even though these are only large, wooden barrels with loose fitting lids, they were all against a wall that collapsed right over the top of them. All the beans and rice and flour are still perfectly good.

After several more hours of digging, I'm pretty sure that we've found nearly all the food. Of course, with all the muck, we can't be sure. But we've found enough to feed La Rupa for many weeks. This is the good news.

The bad news is that even with all this food, in our wet, rainy, muddy, world of water, water and more water – we don't have anything to drink.

Ten

There's no safe tap water in La Rupa because the sewer pipes burst and contaminated it. The creek, which runs on the south side of town, is now more mud than liquid. The only flush toilet left in La Rupa is in our house, but there's no running water and the sewer line's broken so it doesn't flush anymore. The Rodriquez family has an outhouse, but it's useless too. Raw sewage is oozing up out of the mud in the streets. It stinks.

With water so scarce, we collect rain in bottles, pots and pans, plastic bags, and every other container we can find. But this water is used up as quickly as it's collected. If the rain stops for very long, we'll be in serious trouble. We have no way of storing a large amount of water anyway. I don't know what we're going to do.

★   ★   ★

Alfredo Menendoz, my friend from outside of town, returns with a box of canned tomatoes and a large bag of ground corn flour. He looks relieved to see our supplies of food; his family is probably sharing more than they can really afford to share. He's already sent some of our neighbors back to his house to stay.

Most importantly, though, Alfredo tells me that they have a large water tank, and that it's overflowing from all the rain. Alfredo promises to tell his father about our water shortage, and that they'll help us. We can share some of our food and they can share water.

Alfredo asks me, 'What is this smell?'

I answer, 'We think it is mostly the sewage.'

'Mostly?' Alfredo asks.

'Well,' I say softly, 'there are a lot of dead people in the mud too.'

Alfredo looks embarrassed and shocked, 'Yes, of course,' he says quickly, 'I'm sorry.'

I say, 'It was good of you to bring this food. You should take some of our canned things back in trade.'

'Oh no,' Alfredo says, 'we're all right.'

'So are we, Alfredo, so you must take your share.'

I hand him a canned ham and several cans of fruit and milk.

'This is plenty,' Alfredo insists. 'When we need more I'll come get it. Some of the people who are back home with me now can bring some water back here.'

'OK,' I agree.

It's too bad that the Menendoz house, with its water is so far away, but we're lucky that it's there at all.

With so much to do and so much to think about, I've kept my worries about Dad and Victor and Ruby to a minimum over these last few hours. But as another night comes, and I go to bed, my mind begins to wander and I start worrying again.

At some point, I finally fall asleep. Victor and I are building a barbecue on the beach at Omoa. The blue water of the Caribbean laps the shore, and clouds, puffy and white and harmless drift in the bright blue sky.

Victor says, 'We'll need this for the storm. The mud will not hurt us, you know.' I know exactly what he's saying and I work eagerly and happily with him even though a big brick barbecue in the middle of a white beach, with no house, no hut; nothing anywhere near us, doesn't really make much sense.

Out splashing and swimming in the water is Ruby. She looks so beautiful.

'You're beautiful,' I yell; somehow it doesn't feel funny or awkward to say this to my sister, something I'd *never* say in real life.

Ruby puts her hand up to her ear, signaling that she can't hear me, and then she laughs and dives under the water.

My father walks up to us, carrying three huge, lovely lobsters. 'La Ceiba crawdaddys,' he says and laughs.

I say, 'But there're only three!'

Dad smiles and says, 'Three is all we need. Three's plenty.'

For some reason, I begin to cry. I'm embarrassed and ashamed of my tears. But Victor turns to me and says, gently, 'It's all right, Jose. It's OK to be sad, but don't worry, this barbecue will save you all – don't worry, Jose.'

Now, I know that I'm dreaming because I can't imagine Victor *ever* giving me permission to weep. As I think this thought, Victor stops his work and looks straight at me there are tears in his eyes too. 'We all weep sometimes, Jose. It's OK.'

I wake up to a terrible rattling sound. At first, still half asleep, I wonder if it's one of the lobsters from my dream, scratching his claws against the red bricks of the barbecue. But now I realize that this rattling sound, horrible, loud and gasping, is my little brother Juan trying to breathe.

Eleven

It's been three long, horrible days and nights since La Rupa was destroyed, but all I can think about this morning is Juan's skin color. It's more the shade of the dead than of the living. A few days ago, I was just a normal kid, now I'm an expert on the color of death.

Mom holds Juan and rocks him quietly. By pretending to be calm, she tries to quiet his fears, but he looks scared and sick. We can't find the thermometer to take Juan's temperature, but we know he has a high fever. One moment he sweats and the next he shakes and quivers from chills. His breathing is labored and marked by the terrible rattling sound.

I'm scared. My hands shake. I feel like crying, but it's different than before. Staring at poor little Juan, my tears are those of rage and frustration. I feel like screaming at God, cursing, tearing at my own flesh, or pulling out my hair. I can barely catch a breath. My heart pounds so loud inside me that I wonder if others can hear it. I need to save Juan. I'd do anything to help him. He's so small and weak, but—

'What can I do?' I desperately ask my mom.

'I don't know,' she answers quietly. 'We need a doctor.'

'Yes,' I answer quickly. Of course, a doctor, a doctor. 'I'll go get one,' I say, louder than I mean for the words to be.

'In San Pedro?' my mother asks.

'Yes.' I answer, forcing my voice to be quieter.

'How will you get there?'

'I'll run,' I say calmly, and I'm already on my feet, moving towards the door.

'But the bridges, the flooded roads—' Mom begins.

I interrupt, 'I'll be careful, but I'm *going*!'

Mr Barabon says that he'll watch over Mom and my sisters. I can't even look at Juan who seems half-dead already. I grab an empty, plastic soda pop bottle, the kind with a twist top, full of drinking water. I don't need anything more, San Pedro is only thirteen miles away – either I'll make it, or— I head out the front door.

I begin to run down the street. I'm sinking into the mud but I ignore this. I'm running as hard as I can, towards the highway south of town. I force myself to slow down, to pace myself, but running is the only thing I can do to take my mind off of Juan.

Twelve

I've traveled this route to San Pedro Sula on a bus every school day of my life, so it should be familiar to me. But it's so different now. What was once lush forest and green pasture is now mud and water; brown and brackish and never-ending. Once I'm out of view of La Rupa, I can barely tell which direction to go. The few patches of road not buried in mud are covered in muddy water – over and over again, I slip off the pavement and feel my ankle turn.

Where am I? Which way La Rupa? Which way San Pedro? Fear starts to take over, my breaths coming faster and faster – soon I'm panting, not from exhaustion, but from being so afraid. I can't tell where I am. I stop, and search the landscape for some landmark, or some sign that might help me know which way to go.

Shivers run through my body and I feel like I'm about to start crying again. I'm furious at my cowardice – what would Victor do right now? I know what he *wouldn't* do, he wouldn't stand here shaking with fear. But if I'm lost, what will happen to Juan? If I can't find my way, what will happen to me?

I move on, but nothing looks familiar – the trees that used to line the road are either washed away or so bent and broken that they could be any trees, anywhere. I think I'm going the right way, though, because I keep feeling the road under my feet. But is this the right road? Could I have wandered on to one of the side roads that lead in the wrong direction?

I think about little Juan, so sick and pale, about my mom waiting for me to bring back help, about Dad and Victor and Ruby, maybe dead. No! They can't be dead. They're alive. We just don't know where they are.

The brown water comes up over my ankles and in some places nearly reaches my knees. I worry that if Dad and Victor and Ruby *are* dead, if they are drowned, they could be near me right now, under this muddy water – on my next step, I might bump into one of their bodies, stinking and bloated, like the bodies back in La Rupa. I take small steps, afraid of what my feet might hit as I walk.

I'm so afraid – afraid of going forward, afraid of turning back. I'm not even sure which way *is* forward.

Finally, I see the Ochoca bridge in the distance. It's three miles outside La Rupa, the bridge to the highway and to San Pedro Sula. The Ochoca bridge means I'm going the right way, and that I'm not lost. But as I get closer I see that there is no Ochoca bridge any longer, and the Ochoca river, which has always been a slow, lazy, little creek, has become a roaring, muddy torrent.

The gray, concrete pillions, on which the bridge used to sit, are still here, scarred and battered, but the bridge itself, the girders and the large railings along with the asphalt roadway are gone. I stand on the bank and look at the muddy water – it doesn't look especially deep but it's moving really fast. I don't like the thought of trying to wade across on foot. To force my courage up, though, I think about little Juan as I make my way down the embankment.

It's raining again, a steady drizzle, irritating and chilly. I stand on the shore and look up and down the river. This place looks like as good a spot as any to try and get across. I'm trying to decide whether to take off my shoes or not, when I look up and see the carcasses of a man, cat and a dog floating by. The man, thank God, is not Victor or my dad or anybody else I recognize. He is floating face down. His body looks like a log or some other bulky thing. But his arms are outstretched in death, his hands brownish black. The cat, an orange tabby, is puffed up and bloated while the dog, black, looks flat and deflated. It's strange to see them all float past together. A dead man. A dead cat. A dead dog. Death. Were they once friends in life? Family? Did they die together? It's almost ridiculous. It's almost a joke. I've never seen anything like this before. How much death is down there on the murky riverbed? Dad? Victor? Ruby? I can't see into the water; it's far too muddy. I try to shake these thoughts away, but I decide to keep my shoes on.

I'm ready to take my first step into the current, when I'm stopped in mid-stride by a sudden, surprising sight and sound. Roaring and splashing into the river, from the opposite bank, only a few dozen yards downstream is a camouflage colored military vehicle marked *United Nations Relief*. Another vehicle just like it follows, and then a third truck with a Red Cross logo on its side and hood. All three trucks splash into the river and begin to power their way across.

For a moment, I just stand here. The splash of the first vehicle sprays out, showering the carcasses of the man and cat and dog, as they float past. Suddenly I realize that the Red Cross means that this is a *medical* truck! They can help Juan!

I run along the bank, waving my arms. The soldiers in the first vehicle don't see me. I panic, still running and trying to think of the words for what I need.

I wave my arms more frantically, almost falling down and begin to holler, 'My brother is sick!' I yell this as loud as I can, first in Spanish, and then in English. 'My brother is sick!' Stumbling over the round river rocks, my heart pounds in my chest and I can barely hear my own voice over their roaring engines.

The two men in the first vehicle still don't see me, but I look at the driver of second vehicle, and at a man and woman in the third truck. They stare straight at me.

As they come out of the river, the second and third vehicles stop and honk their horns to the lead vehicle. The first vehicle stops abruptly too. Blue exhaust pours out from their exhaust pipes and steam rises from around the engines.

I run up to the second vehicle and say in English, 'My brother is sick! Can you come help?'

The soldier sitting in the passenger seat says, 'You speak English?' he sounds surprised, even a little pleased. But he doesn't sound American. His accent is strange to me.

'Yes,' I answer, 'I'm a student at the International School, I am English, very well.'

'S'cuse me?' The soldier smiles.

I realize my mistake and quickly add, 'I haven't spoke English since the storm came. I am a little . . . for a moment . . .' I can't think of the word.

'Rusty?' the soldier asks.

'Exactly,' I say and force myself to smile. 'Yes, rusty, I am usually good at speaking English, but I am rusty just a little now.'

'You're doing fine,' the driver says. Then he asks, 'You've got a brother who's sick?'

'Yes!' I say, too loudly, almost yelling, 'My little brother Juan is very sick! Are you a doctor?'

'I'm not, but Captain Albertson is. He's in the next rig back. I'm not sure we can help you though, son.'

My heart sinks. Not help? How could that be? My mouth goes dry and I can't think of a single word in

English. But if this Captain is a doctor, surely he will help; surely he *has* to help!

'But my brother is *very* sick,' I say, trying but unable to keep the fear out of my tone. 'Dead,' I say, blurting the word out, 'there are many dead and my brother will dead . . . I mean . . . my brother will be dead if I don't bring help.'

'Talk to the Captain, lad,' says the soldier in the passenger seat.

I hurry back to the third vehicle, the one with the red crosses on it. A woman soldier is driving and a man soldier with gold bars on his shoulders sits next to her. They are both light-skinned. He has a kind face, which is good because he is a *huge* man – he's twice my height and three times my weight. He has red hair and blue eyes and freckles on his fingers, which makes him look young.

Finally, I force myself to speak, 'Are you the Captain Doctor?'

'Yes,' he answers kindly; he smiles at me with white teeth, 'You speak English?'

He doesn't sound American either – he sounds strange, like the soldiers in the other truck. I ask, 'Where are you here from away?'

He smiles and says, 'We're with the UN International Relief Force; our squadron is international, but I'm from the UK.'

Quickly I say, 'My brother is very sick, he needs help right away!'

'I'm sorry,' the doctor says, 'But we're under strict orders . . .'

I interrupt, 'But my brother is just a baby—'

I feel tears building up in the back of my throat and at the corners of my eyes. I fight the tears back; I must stay calm and convince this man to come and help us. I can barely breathe but I force myself to stay calm. What would Victor do? What would Dad say?

'I'm sorry,' the doctor says again, and I can tell that he truly *is* sorry. 'But we're under strict orders to go to— Where?' He turns to the lady soldier who is behind the steering wheel of the jeep.

She says, 'Las . . . Las Ruppa?' pronouncing it wrong.

'La Rupa?' I ask.

'Yes,' the doctor says, 'La Rupa, do you know where it is?'

'Yes,' I say quickly, 'Yes, I know *exactly* where La Rupa is.'

Thirteen

In the truck, I tell them what has happened; about the rains, the power failure, the mudslide, the water, the food, the Arroyos and all the other dead, and about my brother Juan. I try to speak slowly and clearly, and I struggle to remember all the right words in English.

The doctor says, 'Jesus.'

Now he tells me about San Pedro Sula and the rest of Honduras; about the town of La Lima being buried in water, thousands of people waiting on the road to be rescued; about the Bay Islands and the horrible damage there. He tells about the shelters all across Honduras overflowing with people, so many homeless, and about some children who sat on a rooftop for three days and nights, no food, no water, after their parents were swept away by the floods.

He says, 'People in La Ceiba are fishing from their front porches, actually catching fish and crawdads from what used to be the streets.'

When he mentions La Ceiba, I think about my father and Victor and Ruby. I tell him about them, rambling on, crazy-sounding, about Victor and his barbecue, Ruby and her modeling portfolio, my dad and his truck. I realize that I must sound crazy.

As I finish I say, 'Of course, maybe they are all right. Maybe they are staying with people somewhere. Maybe they are—'

I begin to sob. It flies out of me, like when you throw-up suddenly. Snot runs from my nose and I turn my head away to stare out the window of the jeep so that these soldiers won't see me. I'm embarrassed.

The doctor asks, 'What kind of truck does your father drive?'

'A medium-sized one,' I say.

I hear the doctor's soft smile in his voice, 'No Jose, I mean, what make, what model, what color is it?'

I explain, 'It is a white, Volvo truck, a large van – it is four years old, a 1994, perhaps a '93?'

'Very good Jose,' the doctor says. He picks up the

microphone attached to the radio that is suspended from the dashboard of the jeep.

'This is MEDRUN 89er – come in.'

The radio crackles back, 'Acknowledge MEDRUN 89er – identify.'

'Captain Albertson, Unit 89.

'Acknowledge – state your purpose, Sir.'

Captain/Doctor Albertson speaks clearly and directly, an official sound to his words, 'We're approximately three kilometers outside the village of Las Rupa. Have encountered and enlisted support of English speaking Honduran national to assist in translation. Over.'

'Copy that, Sir. Over.'

'Need an all-alert priority, search and seek, three Honduran nationals, Identities: Senor . . .'

He pauses a second, letting his thumb slip off the button on the microphone. He turns to me, 'What is your father's full name?'

'Albert,' I say, then quickly I correct myself, 'Alberto Cruz.'

The doctor clicks the button of the microphone again, 'Senor Alberto Cruz and two adult children . . .'

The doctor passes the rest of the information along.

The radio crackles again, 'Copy all and roger that, Sir. Good luck in La Rupa; it sounds pretty ugly out there.'

The doctor glances at me, a flicker of embarrassment crosses his face. 'Affirmative. We'll check back at 1100 hours and provide update on mission status. Signing off.'

'Signing off, Sir.'

The radio static goes silent.

I don't know what to say, other than, 'Thank you, Doctor, thank you so much.' I fight back tears again, tears of gratitude.

'It's the least we can do for our new translator,' the doctor says, his voice kind and gentle. 'You will help us, right?' he asks.

'Absolutely,' I answer, 'of course!'

The lady soldier who is driving the truck leans over and looks around the doctor's huge body. She smiles at me. She's tall too, not gigantic like the doctor, but taller than Honduran women. She has a pretty face.

We arrive at the southern entrance to La Rupa. As the vehicles slowly inch forward, I am stunned, once more, by the devastation; I can't get used to it. We move past the Rodriquez's little shack. The people standing and sitting there watch us in silence. No one looks surprised to see me in the vehicle with these soldiers, no one looks happy or scared or anything really, just numb. Some of the people get to their feet and begin to walk cautiously towards us. They remind me of zombies again; they look like they looked in my house, after we gave up digging for bodies. It's almost impossible to still see my neighbors and friends in the faces of everyone. A few months, a few *days* ago, these people were like family. I remember when they cheered Victor's barbecue. Now, they seem kind of like ghosts.

Silently, I say a prayer for Dad and Victor and Ruby and then as we look out at what's left of La Rupa, I feel a terrible sick feeling. I say another prayer for Juan; a prayer that he's all right, and that we aren't too late to help him. My heart pounds. Please be all right Juan!

Fourteen

We stop the truck where the mud makes it impossible to drive any further. How long until the doctor can see Juan? Has the fever stolen his last breath? I try to mentally will the doctor to hurry up the muddy street to our house.

As we get out of the truck, Dr Albertson asks, 'Where is your brother?' He's such a huge man, and standing up out of the truck, he casts a shadow as big as a building or a tree.

'That is our home,' I answer, pointing up the street, 'Juan is there with my mother and many more people.'

'Let's go!' Dr Albertson snaps.

As we walk, Dr Albertson calls his nurse, Lieutenant Sally. They talk quietly as we hurry up the muddy road. They wear boots that come up over their ankles and have thick treads on the bottom, so they pass through the mud much more quickly than I can. I struggle to keep up.

They pause at the door to my house, waiting for me.

I'm breathing hard as I step past them and walk into the living room. Everybody looks up at me and at the huge doctor and the nurse.

I say in Spanish, 'This is Captain Doctor Albertson and Lieutenant Nurse Sally, they've come to help us. They don't speak Spanish, but I'll help.'

I glance around and see that my mother and Juan are not here. A bad feeling rushes through me – where are they? I begin to sweat and I feel dizzy. 'Where's Juan?' I want to ask but the words, jumbling up in English and Spanish, stick in my throat – where's my brother? My mom?

Suddenly Mom, carrying Juan on her hip, steps into the room from her bedroom. Juan looks pale and tired, but he's awake and quiet; he stares straight at us. In his right hand he carries C3PO. I smile at Juan but his eyes look glassy. He doesn't smile back.

'Pneumonia,' Doctor Albertson says to me, then he quickly adds, 'I think he'll be OK. I've given him enough antibiotics to cure a whole village. In situations like this, where there is so much dampness and dirt, bronchitis and pneumonia are quite common. But your little brother is strong and we got to him early. He needs bed rest and liquids but I think he'll be OK'.

My eyes sting again; I've never felt like crying so much.

'You did well, Jose,' Nurse Sally says, 'I'm glad you found us and helped us to get here. Good work.'

For some reason, her kind words make me even more emotional. But I refuse to cry in front of them again, these new friends, these lifesavers. I force myself to think about the work ahead, about all of the people who need the doctor's help.

I mutter, 'I'm just glad you were coming here.'

Doctor Albertson seems to blush. Watching him work with Juan, the doctor's hands look huge as he gently takes Juan's tiny arm and lifts it up. The doctor's hands look like they could lift the whole world. He wears a plain gold wedding band, a huge ring; it would be way too big for my thumb. It looks more like a bracelet. Dr Albertson says to me, 'It's lucky we met you. The translator for our team, Sergeant Hernandez, is on medical leave, his wife is having a baby – he'll be catching up with us next week, but in the meantime we weren't sure how we were going to manage. We're a multi-national UN team: Sergeant Broussard is French and understands a little bit of Spanish, Corporal DiAmanti is Italian and speaks a little, all of us communicate together in English, but none of us but Sergeant Hernandez are fluent in Spanish. You've helped us as much as we've helped you.' The doctor's kind words are too kind. This man saved little Juan. He can do no wrong in my eyes.

Now the doctor asks me to translate his words to my mother.

'Mrs Cruz, you have good boys here,' he says, smiling.

I'm a little embarrassed to translate this.

The doctor sees my hesitation, 'Tell her exactly what I said, Jose.'

I follow his orders and my mother smiles and nods to him.

He says, 'Mrs Cruz, you've done a wonderful job helping your neighbors, now I need to ask you to do even more.'

Dr Albertson pauses to allow for my translation to catch up. Mom nods to him as I talk. When I've finished speaking he adds, 'Your home looks like the only secure structure in Las Ruppa. We need to set up an emergency clinic here; is that agreeable to you?'

As I finish my translation, Mom nods and says in Spanish, 'Of course.'

'Thank you, ma'am,' Dr Albertson says.

As I watch this English doctor and my mom talk, I'm surprised at how strong and brave my mother is. Here is this huge soldier, and here is mom, all of five feet one inch in height, yet she looks straight at him as he speaks. Even though Mom doesn't speak English, she listens carefully to him, watches his expressions and then listens equally carefully to my translations of his words. Watching the two of them, I see something in my mother that I've never seen before; a courage and assurance, strength and confidence. She says nothing about Dad and Victor and Ruby, shows nothing of the worry I know she's feeling.

The doctor and Nurse Sally begin to move people from one side of the room to another, and Nurse Sally calls out to the other soldiers to hurry and bring up the medical supplies.

'You're first,' Nurse Sally says to me.

Surprised, I answer, 'Why? I'm fine – I'm not hurt.'

'Oh really,' Nurse Sally says, 'and these wounds are normal for you?'

I look at the red spots she points to on my arms and ankles, at the cuts, scratches and ugly splotches on my skin. I honestly hadn't even noticed them until this moment.

Nurse Sally speaks loudly enough so that Dr Albertson will hear her; 'The doctor will tell you these splotches are impetigo, and about the importance of cleaning up the cuts and abrasions, especially with so much infection possible. Doctors love to think that they're the only ones who know such things.'

I hear and see Dr Albertson chuckle at her words. He stands at the new 'pharmacy' in the corner of our living room, and says over his shoulder, 'And nurses, especially when they are out-ranked, love to think that they know as much as their superiors.'

Nurse Sally laughs, too. 'Superiors,' she says quickly, 'You heard that, didn't you, Jose? "Superiors", you're my witness. Ah, doctors, they have such wonderful fantasy lives.'

And so it goes, back and forth between them.

They give me medicine for my skin, and then Nurse Sally cleans and disinfects the many scratches and small cuts that cover my hands, forearms and ankles. She is very gentle and the medicine hardly hurts.

When they have finished treating me, I translate for them as they begin helping everyone else.

Mr Barabon gets bandages for his cut and bruised hands. Translating for him, he says nothing about his two dead children. Mr Handel is the same, his back is bent and his ankle is black and blue, horribly swollen, yet he says nothing about these injuries, nor does he mention losing his wife.

After a while everyone in the village is lined up, sitting or standing quietly, in front of our house, waiting to see the doctor.

The children get shots, none of them crying, not even the little ones like Alberto Handel or Miguel Cortez, both of whom lost their moms in the mudslide.

Dr Albertson says to each patient, 'If you get an infection or become sick, it might be a while before we can get back here. You must stay healthy.'

Nurse Sally tells everyone 'Boil, boil, boil, your water, unless it comes straight from a bottle.'

The day drags on. As I translate, I notice that no one, not any parent who has lost a child, nor any child who has lost a parent or brother or sister, not a single person complains. A few of the injuries are more serious, broken hands, wrists, fingers, but most are things like sprains of every type from ankles to shoulders to knees, and the beginnings of sickness, bad coughs and runny noses – still, no one complains, no one loses their dignity. I realize how selfish I've been to be so concerned just with Juan or with my dad and Victor and Ruby, but I still feel the same way and couldn't act any different if I tried.

When we are finally finished with the last patient, one of the other soldiers comes in to talk with Dr Albertson. I use the break to go to the front door and look out at the town. The soldiers who were in the first two trucks have set up large tents. From where I'm standing, with the sides of these tents rolled up, I see that these temporary shelters have cots and cooking stoves, stacked up metal cans of cooking fuel and big bottles of water, and packets of food. These are shelters for all the people who have been staying with us, the Rodriquez family and with Alfredo's family. With a little sharing between families, there are enough large tents for everyone who needs them. These soldiers have shown us that we are not alone, that La Rupa has not been forgotten.

When I step back into the room, I overhear the soldier say to Dr Albertson that there is nothing more they can do today and that they need to head back to San Pedro Sula for the night. Dr Albertson agrees but turns to me and promises that they'll come back again, 'later in the week, next week at the latest'. They've done so much for us.

But now that everything that can be done for the living is done, I hear them say that it's time to take care of the dead.

Fifteen

Some bodies might never be found. They are buried too deep or have been swept too far away. But some bodies have pushed up to the surface, a hand, a foot, a rib cage, a spine barely covered by flesh, these horrors fill the spaces where homes once stood. To make things worse, there's no chance for proper burials and services. The soldiers tell us, just before they leave, that the Honduran Military will come later today to help us.

Just before nightfall, the Honduran soldiers arrive – the death detail. They come in four beat-up old Honduran military trucks. They've brought with them two small tractors and a backhoe to retrieve all of the dead bodies they can find.

The tractor's engines sputter to life, the backhoe moves slowly towards where the Cortez house used to be. I smell the wafting blue diesel smoke. We stand by quietly and watch as the empty ground where houses once stood is torn up, gathering the dead bodies.

The machines don't stop until ten o'clock in the night. Then, they haul the dead to a field southwest of town, a quarter mile away. The winds are blowing from the northeast. The soldiers have picked the spot where they will burn the bodies.

One of the Honduran soldiers, the last one still in town, speaks to me. 'Did you lose anyone here?' he asks gently. He is a young guy, maybe Victor's age. He has darker skin than I do, and his features look Indian. He's handsome and his voice is kind. Even though he's just a kid, he looks grown-up in his dark green Honduran Army uniform. We're alone by the trucks. The rest of the villagers have gone back into their tents and shelters. The other soldiers are at the fire.

I answer his question, 'No, I have no dead family here, just friends and neighbors.'

I add, 'My father and older brother and older sister are missing.'

He looks away from me and says, 'I'm sorry.'

'Yeah,' I answer. Then I quickly add, 'We still hope to hear from them.'

'Of course,' the young soldier nods, but he still doesn't look into my eyes.

I ask, 'How do you burn the bodies?'

I feel embarrassed that I've asked such a blunt question, but he takes it in his stride.

'We use kerosene, douse them real good and set the torch.'

'It must be very difficult.'

He hesitates a moment and then says, 'If this were Tegoose, it would be hard. That's where I'm from, and if these were my people, people I know, I couldn't do it. But here, and on the roadside where we burn the bodies from the rivers and fields – I don't think of them as people. They're just bodies, you know, not even bodies, just dead things, nothing . . .'

Suddenly he stops and looks into my eyes, 'I'm sorry,' he says, 'I didn't mean—'

I interrupt him, 'No, it's OK, I understand; you're doing a hard job and you're helping us. Don't feel bad.'

The soldier nods.

'I have to go,' he says. 'They need the rest of this kerosene.'

Kerosene, for burning the bodies.

'Sure,' I say.

I watch him walk towards his truck, climb up and glance back at me. I yell over the rumbling of his truck's engine, 'Good luck and thanks.'

He smiles, and waves goodbye.

As I watch him drive away, I think about what he just said about burning the bodies they find in the rivers and the fields. I think about the radio reports of the missing. There are 'many *thousands* of missing people'. How many of these people will never be found, if their bodies are pulled from the rivers and fields and burned without positive identification? I try to force myself away from these thoughts – but I keep thinking of Dad and Victor and Ruby, *missing, missing, missing*. I can barely breathe. Where are my father, my brother and my sister? Are they lost forever? Are they still alive?

I try as hard as I can to catch a deep breath, but it won't come. Missing! '*We burn the bodies we find in the rivers and fields . . .*'

I am so tired. I ache, inside and out. Everything hurts: my legs and my arms, my stomach and back and chest, even my teeth and my fingernails – every part of my body is sore. Yet, all I can think about is my father and brother and sister, *missing*. Until I know what's become of them, I won't care how much I hurt.

Sixteen

In the darkness, Mom, Angela, Maria, and I stand on
our porch. Mom put Juan to bed and he's asleep already,
but the rest of us watch the yellow, orange flames of the
soldier's fire to the south.

After a while, I notice that Maria has moved closer to
me. I can't remember the last time I spoke to Maria –
Hours? Days? Never?

Maria says softly, 'They aren't burning life. They're
burning death.'

I look at her and put my arm around her shoulders.
'You're right Maria.' As I hold her, she slips her arm
around my back. I can't think of another time in our
lives when Maria and I have held each other like this. It
feels good. As the next oldest to me in age, Maria is to
me like Ruby was to Victor. *IS* to Victor!

Angela and Mom stand quietly. Our friends and neighbors, who slept here the last two nights, are now in the big green tents that the soldiers put up for them. We have our home back for ourselves.

Looking at the fire in the distance, Mom says, 'Pray for them, for their souls.'

Angela asks, 'What should I say? What words?'

'Whatever words your heart tells you. Or the Rosary, pray what feels right to you.'

Maria begins to whisper softly, *'Our father who art in heaven, hallowed be thy name . . .'*

I pray, *God, if you're really there, if you're listening . . .*

I get nervous. Is this any way to talk to God? But I can't stop myself,

I don't know why you sent us this. I don't understand?

This is no way to talk to God. I try again . . .

Our Father who art in heaven, hallowed be thy name. Thy kingdom come, thy will be done . . .

Where is *my* father who is on earth? . . .

On earth as it is in heaven . . .

Why did this happen God? Where's Dad? Victor? Ruby?

I pause, wondering if God might be mad at me for what I'm saying. I try again . . .

*Our father who art in heaven, hallowed be thy name, give
us this day . . .*

No, that's wrong, that's not how it goes. I'm so tired,
so confused that I can't even say it right.

Please Jesus, please God help all our friends. I pray for the
Arroyos; I pray for all the dead people, that God will give
them peace . . . I pray for Ruby and for Victor and Dad.

My head aches from trying to pray. Mom told us to
pray for the dead, yet I'm praying for Dad and Victor
and Ruby. They're not dead! Maybe they aren't – NO,
they can't be dead . . . God, please let Dad and Victor
and Ruby be all right . . .

*Our father who art in heaven, hollow be thy name . . . no,
I mean 'hallowed', not 'hollow' . . . I'm sorry . . .*

*God, please, I'm asking you, please just let my family be
all right!*

Is God making sense out of my prayers? Does
anything make sense any more?

I watch the flames against the dark sky, the bodies of
La Rupa burning.

In bed, an hour later, I feel so tired. My limbs ache. My
hands hurt. Even my eyelids sting. Luckily, I fall asleep
right away.

My dreams are confused. Some are nice, like seeing Ruby eating an apple and laughing at something Dad has said. Mom laughs too. This actually happened in real life, just like this – Ruby and the apple, Dad and Mom – just like in this dream, everything just the same.

In my next dream, Victor stands next to me at the barbecue, pointing at the huge rock jammed against the back.

'What the hell is this?' Victor asks angrily.

I answer, 'Don't swear in your prayers, Victor.'

Victor points at the barbecue again, at a dozen or so bricks knocked off by the boulder, 'We'll have to fix this.' Then, smiling at me he adds 'Hail Mary full of grace . . . Damn it!' Victor laughs loudly.

I have lots more dreams about my family, and when I wake up this morning only one thought is on my mind – I have to find Dad and Victor and Ruby; I have to find them!

Mom says, 'No! Absolutely not! You're not leaving again! Can't you see how much I need you here?'

Of course, I know she's right, but I'm crazy with worry.

'I'll be careful. I'll come back every night, but I have to look for them. Maybe they're hurt! Maybe they need my help! I have to try.'

Mom says, 'The soldiers are looking for them. They have helicopters, trucks, hundreds of people. What can you do that they aren't doing already?'

I say, 'I can search for *my* family. I know the soldiers mean well, but they have too much to do. They don't know us. They won't search the way that I will.' I don't tell Mom what I'm really most afraid of, that the soldiers might find their bodies, Dad and Victor and Ruby, and not know who they are and just burn them – if that happened, we'd never know for sure what happened to them. Thinking this thought makes me crazy.

Mom's quiet a moment. Then she says softly, 'You may be right Jose, I know you would try hard to find them, but I *need* you here.' I look at her face. Something's changed between us, a new kind of trust.

I say, 'You're right.' But then I add, 'I'll wait a little while, another day or two until things are better.'

Although neither of us says it out loud, we both know that nothing will be 'better' in a 'day or two'. We see this in one another's eyes. We're both right – I should be out searching for Dad and Victor and Ruby *and* I need to stay here in La Rupa with Mom, helping her. If I do the one good thing, I'll be doing another bad thing, yet if I do the other good thing . . . There's no right answer.

I don't know what else to do, so I pray again. Who am I praying to? What am I praying for? I can't find words that make any sense, so I just mumble prayers over and over. I say a lot of 'Our Fathers'. I wish that I could find words of my own, but they won't come. I pray that somehow everything will be all right. All I have is faith, but I'm afraid I'm running out of it.

Seventeen

After I talk with Mom, later on the morning of this fourth day, a group of us are shoveling mud out of the street so that cars will be able to drive through town again. Mr Barabon, Mr Cortez, and even Mr Ramerez, along with Jorge Alverez, Pablo and Carlos Altunez are with me. Everybody works slowly, shoveling little scoops of mud and drying dirt to the sides of the road. I feel almost good. The blisters on my hands have turned to calluses and I feel strong. It's sunny this morning and the warmth on my shoulders actually feels nice; it reminds me of building the barbecue with Victor, that day when everyone watched us – that seems like a million years ago. The work today, though, helps take my mind off my worries.

The morning passes slowly. Although there isn't much

laughter, we talk softly to one another as we shovel. There's a sense, I think, of doing something, anything we can to get our town back.

Jorge Alverez says to me, 'You were right about the food, about the Arroyos' store. Thank God we had you to show us the way.'

I smile at him. He's only eleven years old, but almost as tall as I am.

I answer, 'I was just lucky. Besides, the Arroyos' store was my mom's idea.'

Mr Cortez overhears us and says, 'No, Jose, luck had nothing to do with it. You are your father's son. You figured out the perfect spot for us to dig. You're smart and hard-working. You're becoming a good man.'

I blush. It feels weird to hear this grown-up talking to me like this, but I've noticed the other grown-ups listening to me too, treating me with respect, like I'm a leader. Maybe this is because our house is the only good building in all of La Rupa. Even though people are sharing the big tents, two or three families per shelter, everyone still comes to our house quite often.

As if he's reading my mind, Mr Barabon says, 'You're the man of your house now, Jose – you're doing a good job.'

I blush again, but say, 'Thanks.'

After digging for a while longer, I hear a vehicle coming into town.

We've made good progress shoveling; we've cleared almost fifty yards, piling the wet, stinking muck on each side of the road. Thanks to all of our work, the visitor, Dr Albertson, is able to drive right up to where we're working. I'm happy to see him again.

He climbs out of his jeep and walks directly towards me.

'*Hola Jose*,' he says.

Although his greeting is warm, when I look at his face, he has a somber expression – in the whole day we spent working together, seeing people with all kinds of sicknesses and injuries, he never looked this sad.

Dr Albertson says, softly, 'We've found the truck.'

At first, I don't know what he's talking about. I ask, 'The truck? You've found the—'

Then it hits me; he means my father's truck.

'Where?' I ask quickly, although I can already tell that something's wrong. My skin breaks out in goose bumps. I feel light-headed. I struggle to get a breath, but force myself to pay attention to his words.

The doctor says, 'It was swept away when the bridge washed out on the Conrejal river just outside La Ceiba.'

'Swept away?' I ask; I don't know the meaning of this English phrase.

The doctor pauses a moment, glances at the ground then back at me, 'The truck was taken by the river when the water knocked down the bridge.'

'Yes,' I say, then I repeat, 'Swept away. What about Dad and Victor and Ruby?'

'They weren't in the truck when we found it, but all the windows were broken out and the rig was submerged.'

'Submerged?'

'Under water.'

We stand together silently. I ask, 'But no sign of them?'

'No,' Dr Albertson answers. 'No sign of anybody, no bodies and no sign of life.'

'Are you sure it's my dad's truck?' I hope that Dr Albertson is wrong.

'There was a MEDRUN support team working only a few hundred yards away from where the truck was spotted. They sent over a patrol. They retrieved some things from the vehicle. You want to look?'

'Things?' I ask, 'Things? Yes, of course.'

We walk to the jeep and the doctor reaches in through the open window and grabs a green, plastic army bag with a zip-lock top. He hands it to me. I open it and look inside.

Immediately, I recognize Ruby's shoe, her low-cut blue cross-trainer. Even through the mud, I see the Nike swoosh stripe; these shoes were Ruby's pride and joy.

I empty the rest of the bag on to the hood of the jeep. There are papers, soaked through and caked with mud, but still partially readable – a registration certificate, insurance documents, a business license in my dad's name, Victor's leather wallet is here too. I pick it up. Although it's wet, it's in almost perfect shape.

My legs feel weak and I feel dizzy, but I manage to mumble something about the condition of Victor's wallet.

Dr Albertson says, 'I noticed that too. I even asked about it. Apparently the wallet was in the jockey box. These other papers,' he points to the soggy mess, 'were attached to the sun visor, that's why they're in such poor condition.'

'Uh huh,' I answer. I leave my hand on the hood of the truck, as wave after wave of nausea rushes through me. Such details, the condition of papers and Victor's wallet, Ruby's shoe, these details are so unimportant, so useless.

Dr Albertson says, 'I'm sorry Jose. To be honest, it doesn't look good. Of course, there's still hope, but realistically, it's not likely that we'll find any bodies. The river's been twenty feet over flood level for so long now. Unless they were seat-belted in, there's no reason they wouldn't have been washed out of the rig. I hate to say this, but I don't see how they could have survived when the bridge went.'

I feel dizzier. And suddenly, I'm falling. I try to grab the jeep's hood, but there is nothing to hold on to. My hand slides along the smooth, green metal.

The doctor reaches over, wraps his huge hand around my arm and steadies me.

'You OK?' he asks.

I nod my head, although I'm not OK at all.

He hesitates, 'I hope I'm wrong, and I certainly could be! Maybe the windows being broken let them escape . . . It's just . . .' He doesn't finish his sentence.

My mother takes the news quietly. Dr Albertson doesn't tell her as many details as he told me. I translate as he explains that the truck has been found but that Dad and Victor and Ruby are still missing.

Mom says, 'We will just keep praying.'

At first, I'm embarrassed to translate this to the doctor. I'm afraid he'll think of us as silly and superstitious. But when I tell him what my mother has said, he nods and takes her hand in his; he says, his voice kind, 'I'll pray too.'

After Dr Albertson leaves, Mom goes quietly back to her chores. I slump down at the kitchen table; stunned, unable to move.

After a while – five minutes? An hour? I have no idea, really – I go out the back door of the house. I stand next to Victor's barbecue. A bad feeling grows inside me. I think about all the prayers I've made, all the 'Our Fathers'. I feel full of hatred and fury. All I wanted was for my family to be OK. All I've asked for, in this rotting world of mud and stench and death, is for God to give me back my family. And this is the answer to those prayers? My chest tightens. My hands turn into fists. My fingernails dig into the flesh of my palms. I shake with anger. I raise my right fist and smash it into the bricks of Victor's barbecue. Pain shoots through my hand and up my arm, but I pull back and hit it again and again. Blood trickles from the open skin on my knuckles. I drag the wounds across the bricks, leaving streaks of smeared blood. I don't even feel sad; I feel like murdering the whole world.

Eighteen

I go back and join the others still shoveling mud from the street, but it's like a fog surrounds me. The others heard what the doctor said about my dad's truck. No one looks me in the eye.

As I shovel, I'm quiet. Mr Barabon and Jorge Alverez, who are shoveling closest to me, must see something in my face that makes them quiet too. We don't speak to each other.

As I work, I think back to a time, last year, when I went with Dad to La Ceiba. All along the road that day, we saw flock after flock of wild parrots, their feathers green, red, and yellow.

'They fly so beautifully,' I said.

'Yes, they really do,' my dad answered me. Then he smiled and added, 'You remember the United

States Super Bowl on TV last week?'

'Sure,' I answered, 'the American Super Bowl, every year in January.'

Dad said, 'Do you think the Super Bowl is as good as our wild parrots?'

I didn't understand his question.

Dad smiled, even laughed a little, 'I don't think the Super Bowl is as beautiful as these parrots. You know?'

We'd watched the Super Bowl game the week before. Actually, Victor and I had watched. Dad had started watching but wandered away. He'd left the house and walked slowly up and down the main street of La Rupa, just chatting with friends and neighbors.

I finally understood what Dad was saying and I returned his smile and answered, 'Yes, you're right, the American Super Bowl isn't as good as our wild parrots.'

As I shovel, the sun warms my shoulders, beats down on my head. I'm sweating. Is this sunshine a message from my father? Is he telling me that wherever he is, everything is all right? Is he telling me that he's somewhere up in the sky, flying with the wild parrots?

Above the hillside is a rainbow. All of the colors are

clear, like streaks of bright paint on a canvas. The reds and greens and yellows remind me of a parrot's wings. Is my dad sending this rainbow?

Now I think about Victor and Ruby, and another memory comes; a couple of weeks ago, I walked into the kitchen and the two of them were sitting at the table munching chips and talking.

'I never said that I "loved" her,' Victor said, laughing as he threw a chip at Ruby.

Grabbing the chip and munching it down, Ruby said to him, 'You didn't have to say it, big boy, look at your face!'

Victor blushed and laughed, 'How am I supposed to look at my face?'

I jumped in, 'You could look in the mirror,' I said.

They both looked at me and burst out laughing.

'What?' I immediately asked, 'What'd I say?'

Victor snarled at me, 'It's just your brilliant problem-solving style, Jose. We're so impressed by your preppy-boy brilliance! I'm glad that Dad is paying those big tuition bills so that you can be so brilliant.'

Ruby looked at me and could see that my feelings were hurt. She punched Victor in the arm and said, 'You stop it,' then she turned to me. 'You're right Jose, he *could* look in a mirror. He's just jealous because you're so smart.'

They both laughed again and, despite myself, I laughed too.

Nobody in the world could make Victor and me laugh the way that Ruby could. I mean the way she *can*. I *won't* give up the hope, however faint that hope might be, that somehow, some way I'll see them again.

I glance at the knuckles on my right hand; tiny splotches of moisture cover the scabbing and the dried blood from where I hit the barbecue. I'm glad that my hand stings, glad that it hurts. The pain is nothing compared to what I feel inside.

It's dinnertime. These last days, despite everything, food has tasted delicious. But today, after the news about dad's truck, I'm not hungry at all; I have no appetite. I move the rice and beans around my plate with my fork and stare at the mess. I'd rather throw this plate against the wall than take another bite, but I know I have to eat. Mom stares at me, but I don't look back at her.

Finally, I manage to eat enough to keep my strength, but I don't taste it. I refuse to enjoy it. I feel bad; my heart is full of hate and anger.

Mom needs me. La Rupa needs me too. But I can't stand the thought of Dad and Victor and Ruby being pulled from the river then burned in a great pile of the unknown. This thought nearly makes me throw up the food I've just choked down.

How could this happen? Why did this happen? One day I was a normal teenager. I liked music and girls and sports. My favorite ice-cream flavor was chocolate cheesecake. I used to go online at school and surf the Internet, imagining that someday I'd travel around the world and see great places. It didn't make any difference where I was *from*. All that mattered was where I was *going*!

But that was then, a thousand years and a million lifetimes ago. Nothing's possible now. How could this have happened to me? How could this have happened to La Rupa?

I refuse to ask God. If Hurricane Mitch isn't God's fault, then God is powerless; if the monster *is* God's fault, then what could I say to God? How can I ever forgive him for taking Dad and Victor and Ruby away? There's nothing God can do now to prove to me that he cares about us.

Nineteen

My sleep is restless and angry. I can't remember my dreams, just a feeling of dread and worry. I wake up more tired than when I went to bed.

It's the fifth day since the mudslide. At least the sun is out again, like it was yesterday. And the electricity is back. It often goes off, but at least we have power part of the time.

The rice and beans and flour we found at the Arroyos' little store, are still kept at our house. Each morning, Mom has Maria and me, with Angela and Juan 'helping', fill plastic bags with this food. Then we kids deliver these bags to the tents and to the Rodriquez place. All the people who were staying out at the Menendoz place have moved back into town, too. They are living in the big tent shelters.

Yesterday, I heard one of the younger kids talking about 'when things get back to normal'. Five days have passed since the earth swallowed thirty-two of us, lives snuffed out in seconds. Those of us who survived, have known nothing but sickness, injuries, and tiredness, our hands and arms and ankles and feet covered in bruises and cuts and scratches, our eyes burning from tears and dirt, our bodies sore and aching – just from trying to stay alive. Half of my family is still missing. 'Back to normal'?

I carry the plastic bags of food to the two tents farthest away from our home and to the Rodriquez place – nine bags in all. Maria and Angela deliver the food to the two tents closer to our house.

I'm walking down the middle of the street, down the wide path we've shoveled clear, when I first hear then see a vehicle coming into town. It's a military truck coming slowly. Lots of trucks have been here over the last few days, so I am not surprised by this one. They could be bringing water, although the water trucks usually don't come 'til later in the afternoon; maybe they're coming to work on the sewer lines or the phones or the electricity, everything still needs work.

As I walk, suddenly a single wild parrot zooms over my head and up towards what's left of the hillside. Most of the time, the wild parrots that live near us are in flocks. This one, flying all alone, surprises me. It lands on a broken tree limb, near the place where the rainbow was when we were shoveling the street. I don't care about wild parrots, anymore, though. What difference do they make? Alone, in a flock, alive or dead, it doesn't matter.

The plastic bags I'm carrying feel heavy, I'll be glad when I'm done with this stupid chore. I kick at a stone that looks like it's just lying in the street, but it doesn't move, part of it's stuck in the ground. For some reason, I'm mad at the rock and mad at myself.

I look back up at the truck still slowly moving towards me. Maybe it's Dr Albertson and Nurse Sally, although even from this distance I can tell that this is a Honduran Army rig, it's older than the UN trucks, spouts blue exhaust from its tailpipe and it moves like a snail. It's still quite a distance away.

Reaching the entrance to the first of my delivery tents, my hands ache from the weight of the bags. I holler into the tent and Elena Barabon, Mrs Barabon, calls back a greeting to me. I step up to the canvas flap door, which she folds open.

I glance back at the truck again, it's closer now, and I can start to make out the occupants. The driver is a young soldier. There are two other people in the cab of the truck. I stare at the passengers.

I don't trust my eyes; I blink and squint, but I keep staring, afraid to look away for even a second. It's dark inside the truck, compared to the bright light of the sunshine, but as a moment passes, I drop all the bags on to the ground. One of them breaks open, spilling rice into the dirt, but I don't even care. I run as fast as I can towards the truck, tripping and almost falling down. I can't believe my eyes. I can't believe what I am seeing!

My heart pounds inside my chest; words catch in my throat! I laugh and yell, not words, just loud hollering all at once!

Seated next to the soldier in the dark truck is my Dad! Beside him – now leaning out the window and smiling at me – is Victor!

Twenty

Tears stream down my face as I reach the passenger door of the truck.

Victor, trying to sound stern, says, 'What're you crying about?' Then he smiles again. I jump up on the running board and Victor puts his hand around the back of my head, grabbing my hair.

Looking past Victor to Dad, I see that his eyes are also filled with tears as he takes his first glimpse of La Rupa since the storm.

'Your mother?' Dad asks. 'Your brother and sisters?'

'Mom's fine. We're all fine. Juan was sick but he's getting better.'

'Thank God,' Dad says softly, then quietly, not really speaking to me, just saying the words out loud, he asks, 'Where's the town?'

* * *

When my dad walks into the house, Mom weeps and laughs; hits him and grabs him, all at the same time. Angela and Juan run to Dad and each lock on to one of his legs, almost toppling him over. Mom hugs Victor.

Maria, standing back a little, asks softly, 'Where's Ruby?'

Her question hangs over the room.

'Ruby's going to be all right,' Dad says. 'She has a broken leg, but the doctor says that it'll mend just fine. She's in a little clinic in Chalupe.'

Dad pauses a moment then says, 'Actually, it was Victor we were worried about . . .'

Smiling and embarrassed, Victor tries to wave off Dad's words. 'It was nothing,' he says, 'a little bump on the head.'

Dad smiles, 'Yes a "little bump", only he was unconscious for three days.'

'I was resting,' Victor says, laughing. But then, 'Actually, I don't know *what I* was doing.'

We gather around the table as Dad explains. They were on the bridge when the water broke over the top. They abandoned the truck and took off on foot. But a huge log, riding the current, rammed into Ruby, breaking her leg and knocking her into the river. Victor dove into the water to save her. But when he came to the surface, he was unconscious.

Dad tells how he pulled them both to safety.

'God was watching over us,' Dad says. 'They surfaced right next to the riverbank.'

Dad carried them, first one for a few steps, then the other, across miles of rain and windswept roadway.

Dad smiles, 'Ruby helped by hopping on one leg. Victor helped by not complaining – but after all, he *was* unconscious.'

We all laugh and Victor smiles.

Dad's voice sounds tired as he tells what happened next, 'We went slowly. The rain was like being hit by stones but luckily the wind was blowing from behind us, pushing us along. I can't even remember very much about the journey, just that I was so worried about Victor and Ruby and that I knew we had to make it to shelter someplace. Finally we got to Chalupe. We've been there all week, no phones, no contact from anyone outside the town until the Honduran military arrived this morning.'

Now it's our turn; we tell Dad and Victor about the monster – the rains, the wind, and the mudslide. We tell about the doctor and soldiers, about finding the food at the Arroyos, about the sewer and phone and water and how I tried to go to San Pedro. But we don't tell them everything; we don't talk yet about the dead.

All of us take turns telling different parts of the story. Mom doesn't say much, she just sits close to Dad and keeps rubbing his arm, touching him and staying at his side.

Finally Juan, looking straight at Victor, says, 'Jose used C3PO, 'cause he was a-scared.'

After Juan says this, he glances quickly at me, apologetically, like his words slipped out by accident.

Victor smiles at Juan and says, 'Yeah, good. It was pretty scary all right.'

Juan smiles at me and I smile back.

Sitting here with my dad and Victor home, knowing that Ruby is alive and safe, I almost feel like a kid again – almost.

I feel a weight lift from my shoulders, an actual physical sensation, like stripping off a heavy coat that's soaked with rainwater. I almost feel light and relaxed and happy – almost. I'd forgotten what this felt like.

But I know that I'm not the same kid anymore. As if reading my mind, Dad says, 'You've done a lot, Jose.'

I answer, 'Everyone has, Dad.'

'Yes, I know,' Dad continues, 'but you've had to be the man here, haven't you?'

Mom interrupts, 'And he's done great.' She leans over, never taking her hand off Dad's arm, and puts her other hand on my shoulder. She kisses my cheek.

I manage not to blush as I wait for Victor to tease me. If there's one thing in the world I can always count on, it's that Victor will never let a compliment go to my head. But Victor's quiet and when I finally find the courage to look over at him, he's smiling at me too. He says softly, 'Sounds like you did pretty good.'

Now I *do* blush, and I say, 'Everyone has done their part, everyone has.' I'm thinking about all of us digging for the dead, digging for food, sharing our water, helping each other in every way we could. But the truth is, looking into Victor's eyes, I *am* proud.

There's a moment of silence at the table. We sit in the glow of being together. The quiet reminds me of saying grace before dinner. I think about that word, 'grace' – Ruby's gracefulness, the grace of God, and the grace of wild parrots flying over La Rupa again.

Author's Note

Hurricane Mitch initially killed more than 5,000 Hondurans. In the months that followed the storm, many of the bodies of the 8,000 'missing' were found. Those missing who were never found are now assumed to be dead.

Mitch was the worst storm in the Caribbean in 200 years. 200 years! The last time Honduras had a storm this bad George III was the King of England.

Floods from Hurricane Mitch affected 70 percent of Honduras' agricultural sector. Entire villages, *entire* villages and *everyone* in them, were wiped out by mudslides. Hundreds of thousands of Hondurans lived for many months in 'shelters.' Many of these shelters were in school buildings, including the school where I had taught, during the year I lived in San Pedro Sula in 1981–82.

Early estimates placed the cost of rebuilding Honduras at $3.8 billion. It may take much more than that.

In many of the small villages, there was no drinking water and the food supplies were dangerously low for months and even years. Dirty water became a breeding ground for mosquitoes. Malaria and dengue were rampant – people's immune systems weaken without enough food, and weak immune systems allowed these diseases to grab hold.

Some people say it could take fifty years for Honduras to 'recover' from Hurricane Mitch. Some say it will take many generations. Like Jose in this story, I don't know how to respond to that kind of talk. 'Recover?' How does one 'recover' from the loss of everything? How does one 'recover' from the loss of somebody, or maybe *everybody*, one has ever loved?

Although this story of Jose Cruz and his family is a work of fiction, it is certainly 'true,' and any resemblance to persons living or dead is absolutely intentional. It is my hope that by telling this story, we might better understand that we live on a relatively small planet and that we're all family. A portion of the proceeds from the sale of this book will be dedicated, through Catholic

Family Charities, to assisting the poor of San Pedro Sula, Honduras and the surrounding region. *Terry Trueman, October 2003*